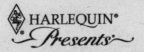

EXPECTING!

She's sexy,
successful...
and
PREGNANT!

Relax and enjoy our fabulous series about
couples whose passion ends in pregnancies...
sometimes unexpected! Of course, the birth
of a baby is always a joyful event, and we can
guarantee that our characters will become
wonderful moms and dads, but what
happened in those nine months before?

Share the surprises, emotions, drama and
suspense as our parents-to-be come to terms
with the prospect of bringing a new baby
into the world. All will discover that the
business of making babies brings with it
the most special love of all....

Delivered only by Harlequin Presents®

Look out for

Pregnant by the Millionaire
by Carole Mortimer
#2568

Coming in February

Lucy Monroe

PREGNANCY OF PASSION

EXPECTING!

She's sexy,
successful...
and
PREGNANT!

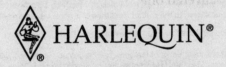

HARLEQUIN®

TORONTO • NEW YORK • LONDON
AMSTERDAM • PARIS • SYDNEY • HAMBURG
STOCKHOLM • ATHENS • TOKYO • MILAN • MADRID
PRAGUE • WARSAW • BUDAPEST • AUCKLAND

ISBN-13: 978-0-373-12590-6
ISBN-10:   0-373-12590-9

PREGNANCY OF PASSION

First North American Publication 2006.

www.eHarlequin.com

Printed in U.S.A.

All about the author...
Lucy Monroe

LUCY MONROE sold her first book in September of 2002 to the Harlequin Presents line. That book represented a dream that had been burning in her heart for years: the dream to share her stories with readers who love romance as much as she does. Since then she has sold more than thirty books to three publishers and hit national bestseller lists in the U.S. and England, but what has touched her most deeply since selling that first book are the reader letters she receives. Her most important goal with every book is to touch a reader's heart, and it is this connection that makes those nights spent writing into the wee hours worth it.

She started reading Harlequin Presents books very young and discovered a heroic type of man between the covers of those books—an honorable man, capable of faithfulness and sacrifice for the people he loves. Now married to what she terms her "alpha male at the end of a book," Lucy believes there is a lot more reality to the fantasy stories she writes than most people give credit for. She believes happy endings are really marvelous beginnings and that's why she writes them. She hopes her books help readers to believe a little, too...just like romance did for her so many years ago.

Lucy enjoys hearing from readers and responds to every e-mail. You can reach her by e-mailing lucymonroe@lucymonroe.com.

To Zachariah, a true knight—
one who is both willing to fight for what is
right and who does it with integrity. You have
my love and admiration always.

CHAPTER ONE

SALVATORE stood outside the small family-owned jeweler's, feeling a wholly unfamiliar wariness.

It wasn't normal for him to hang back from a confrontation. He thrived on the head-to-head combat in the world of big business or the hand-to-hand combat sometimes necessary in his line of work, but this was something entirely different.

It would be a confrontation all right, but it wouldn't be related to business.

He didn't fool himself into believing Elisa would thank him for his interference in her life, even at the instigation of her worried papa. She'd spent a whole year avoiding Salvatore as if he had a particularly deadly communicable disease. She hated him with the same passion she had once given herself to him.

And he could not blame her.

She had more reason than most to despise her ex-lover, but that did not mean he would accept his dismissal from her life. He couldn't. His Sicilian soul would not let such a debt remain outstanding. Even if she did not currently believe it, the di Vitale family was one of honor and he would not bring shame to the name.

He pushed open the door to Adamo Jewelers and frowned when he did not hear the faint buzz that should have accompanied his entry into the store. It was a minimum security measure to alert store employees to a customer's presence.

He took two steps inside and stopped.

She was bending over one of the cases with a young couple. Her soft voice floated toward him even though he could not distinguish her words. Glossy brown hair he remembered best spread across white silk sheets had been pulled into a neat French twist. The conservative style exposed the delicate line of her neck and the faint pulse there that became very visible when she was sexually excited.

She was dressed with her usual flair in a sleeveless button-up blouse, the color of her moss-green eyes. Her straight skirt in a darker shade outlined her slender hips and small waist without showing more than a couple of inches of skin above the ankle. However, if she moved just a little bit, the slit in the back would give him a delicious view of legs he longed to have wrapped around his body in the throes of passion once again.

He gritted his teeth at the predictable reaction to his thoughts occurring below his belt.

He wanted her. Still. He doubted the physical compulsion to merge his flesh with hers would ever diminish. It hadn't in a year of absence. A year in which he had not even been tempted to touch another woman. Such physical desire could make up for a lot…even marriage.

The only course left open to him. The one way he could make reparation for his sins.

She said something to the couple and walked around to the back of the case to pull out a tray of diamond rings.

And saw him.

All the color drained from her face and her eyes, leaving them a bleak winter gray. It was opposite to the reaction she'd once had to his presence, when her eyes had lit up with affection and welcome. There was no welcome now.

No. Horror described her expression best.

The tray tumbled from her hand and landed with a dull thud on the top of the glass case.

"Are you all right?"

Elisa forced her gaze to focus on the man who had just spoken instead of the phantom standing just inside the jewelry store's doorway. She managed to bare her teeth in a semblance of a smile. "Yes. I'm fine."

She straightened the ring tray. "You wanted to look at the marquis-cut solitaire?"

The young woman's eyes lit up and she nodded, turning to her new fiancé with such a look of love, it hurt Elisa to see it. She'd felt that way once.

But Salvatore had destroyed her love as surely as misfortune had destroyed their baby.

Pulling the ring under discussion out of its slot, she made herself smile more genuinely at the couple. It was a good thing to love and be loved in return. The fact that her own life had little hope of such an outcome was no reason to diminish the joy these two were so obviously feeling.

"Why don't you try this on?"

The young man, named David, took the ring and slid it onto his fiancée's finger, his expression tender.

"It fits perfectly," she breathed.

Elisa's smile was not nearly so hard to come by now. That would be another sale. Adamo Jewelers needed it. Desperately.

"It looks beautiful."

She'd almost convinced herself he wasn't there. That he'd been a figment of her imagination—a waking dream…or, rather, a nightmare.

The girl's head came up and she beamed at Salvatore as if he was some sort of benevolent benefactor, when Elisa knew he was anything but.

"Thank you, *signor*."

"From the look of the ring, congratulations are in order, are they not?"

It was David's turn to smile. "Oh, yes. We're going to be married as soon as we get back home."

"Isn't that romantic?" gushed the girl. She looked warmly at her soon-to-be husband. "We met while we were on a European tour. We loved Italy so much, we decided to stay an extra couple of weeks."

"And then we decided to get married." David sounded very satisfied by that state of affairs, his Texas drawl putting emphasis on the word "married."

"Congratulations. I'm sure you'll be very happy," said the man for whom the word "commitment" was considered equivalent to a four-letter word of the worst order.

Elisa ignored him while the couple thanked him for his good wishes, bought the ring and the matching wedding bands that went with it and then left.

After they were gone, she busied herself arranging the jewelry in the case to disguise the hole left by the sold merchandise. She didn't have anything else to put there and wouldn't until after the auction. There were no funds to buy more stones, much less the gold to set them.

"Pretending I'm not here will not make me go away."

She turned and faced him, despising the physical impact his presence even now had on her body.

Her nipples tightened and she felt a reaction in her inmost being she had not had in twelve long months. It was the reaction of her body to its natural mate. Even if her mind and her heart detested him, her body insisted on behaving as if they had been created one for the other.

Not likely.

"Why are you here?" As if she couldn't guess.

She'd lived in Italy most of her adult life and her father was Sicilian. One thing she'd come to realize: Italian guilt was a heavy burden, but Sicilian guilt was even heavier.

And Salvatore had a lot to feel guilty about. More than he knew. More than she would willingly tell him.

Did he want absolution?

He shifted his six-foot-four-inch frame into a leaning position against one of the cases. "Your father sent me."

"Papa?" Her heart contracted. "Is something wrong?"

Dark eyes probed hers and she wanted to close the lids, to protect her inmost thoughts from a man who saw too much while at the same time seeing far too little. He had seen her desire for him, but had not recognized the love. He had seen her reticence about

becoming involved, but had been blind to the innocence that had spawned it.

In the end, he had seen her pregnancy, but not his
own imminent fatherhood in it.

He sighed now, as if what he saw in her eyes bothered him. "Other than the fact you have not come
home in over a year?"

"Sicily is not my home."

"It is where your father lives."

"And his wife."

"Your sister also."

Yes, Annemarie lived with her parents still. Only
three years younger than Elisa's twenty-five years,
Annemarie showed no signs of wanting to move out
and make it on her own in the world. Shawna, Elisa's
mother, would be appalled, just as she had been by
even the slightest inclination to cling shown by her
own daughter.

Elisa had been raised to be fiercely independent.
Her sister had been cosseted in true Sicilian tradition.
"Annemarie will probably live at home until she mar-
ries."

"This is not a bad thing."

Elisa shrugged. "To each her own." She was
pleased with her life in the small town outside of
Rome. Her job allowed her to travel, at least when
there were the funds to do so, and she had no one to
dictate to her. No one at all.

"The announcement buzzer did not go off when I
entered the store."

Trust a security expert to notice. "It's broken."

"It must be fixed."

"It will be." After the auction.

"You have not asked why your father asked me to come."

"I assumed you'd tell me when you were ready. You implied there was nothing wrong with him."

"There is not. If you discount the fear he has for your safety."

Had her father told Salvatore about the crown jewels? She wouldn't put it past him. Francesco Guiliano was a traditional man. Elisa was the result of his one ride on the wild side, an affair with film star Shawna Tyler. He'd wanted marriage when the pregnancy was discovered. Her mother had said no, and meant it. She hadn't wanted a husband to tie her down and had never allowed having a daughter to do so either.

"Why is Papa afraid for me?" She'd been living on her own for seven years.

"He does not believe Signor di Adamo has sufficient security to take possession of something as valuable and controversial as the crown jewels of Mukar."

"That's ridiculous. This is a jewelry store. Of course we can handle having possession of the jewels."

Salvatore moved an impatient hand. "They are worth ten times the entire stock in this place. There is more than one faction in Mukar that is unhappy with the dissolution of the monarchy and the sale of the jewels."

"Mukar needs the working capital. The former crown prince understands that and was willing to make whatever sacrifices were necessary to help his country survive."

"Nevertheless, you are at risk." He sounded so solemn, as if he actually cared.

She almost snorted. Right. Salvatore might feel guilty about the way he'd treated her, but he didn't care about her and she'd be a fool to allow herself the luxury of that fantasy.

"I'm perfectly fine."

"With a broken security buzzer?" He looked around the small jewelry store with a contemptuous eye. "The other security measures here are old and out of date. Even a second-rate thief would have no problem robbing Adamo Jewelers."

"That's not going to happen. There hasn't been a robbery at Adamo's since before Signor di Adamo took over the store and he's in his sixties."

"*Sì*. He is an old man. Too weak to protect you. And times change. You cannot live in ignorance of those changes, even here." He swept his hand out in an arc, indicating the store, but even more so, the small town in which she lived.

"I'm not ignorant!"

He shook his head. "No, but you are dangerously naïve if you believe taking possession of something like the crown jewels of Mukar does not put you at risk."

"I'll be extra-careful. Besides, we keep them locked in the vault."

He shook his head again, his expression grim. "That isn't good enough."

"Whether it is, or it isn't, is none of your business."

"Your father has made it my business."

"He had no right to do that. I run my own life."

She would have said more, but Signor di Adamo

chose that moment to enter the store. He had his grandson, Nico, with him.

"Ah, Signor di Vitale. It is a pleasure to see you again. And this time you visit when my assistant is in town."

"Signor di Adamo." Salvatore turned and extended his hand in greeting, before doing likewise to Nico. "You are getting tall, Nico. Pretty soon you will be working with your grandfather in the store, no?"

Nico beamed with obvious delight and Elisa had to wonder just how much of a friendship had developed between her employer and her ex-lover over the year she'd been avoiding Salvatore.

"If I have a store." The old man's voice lowered with defeat, but then he smiled. "This little girl here, she's given me new hope. Has she told you about the crown jewels?"

"Her father did."

"It is a miracle she convinced the former crown prince to let us handle the auction, but she is smart and pretty enough to convince any red-blooded man of whatever her heart desires." The old man winked at Salvatore. "Is that not so?"

She could have told Signor di Adamo that she hadn't been pretty or desirable enough to convince Salvatore to love her, but she didn't. Because she no longer cared. She didn't want his love. She didn't want his second-hand concern either. She just wanted to be left alone.

She didn't get her wish. Salvatore stayed and discussed the shortcomings in Signor di Adamo's security with the old man. He insisted on doing so in the store, frequently coming into close proximity to her. And every time it happened, the desires of her body betrayed the knowledge of her heart.

It didn't matter what she did to avoid him. She moved to one side of the store and began cleaning jewelry. He followed. The same happened when she went to a jeweler's case on the other side to rearrange its contents. Always it appeared he had been about to move there too, but she felt stalked. Considering the primitive view he had of life, it wasn't hard to imagine him as a predator and herself as the prey.

In less than thirty minutes, her nerves were shot.

Unable to stand the pressure any longer of being around a man she had once loved, who had not loved her and whom she now despised, she sought escape at her desk in the back room. She would work on the auction. Signor di Adamo could man the store.

"You have been running away for a year, Elisa. That is over."

Stupid. She castigated herself mentally as the voice she was trying so desperately to avoid attacked taut nerve endings. It had been really dim to take refuge in the small confines of an office that had only one exit. She faced him, wishing for the numbness she had felt for so many months after the death of her baby and the destruction of her dreams.

He stood blocking that exit—his head almost brushing the top of the doorframe, his shoulders filling it.

She refused to allow any of the emotions roiling inside her to show on her face. "I'm not running. I have work to do."

"So, it has not been running when you manage to be gone every time I have come to visit."

"I wasn't always gone."

"No, this is true. The first time I came, you were home in your apartment, but you refused to open the door."

She'd threatened to call the police if he didn't go away and she'd meant it. Even so, she had not expected him to leave, but he had. A male of his wealth and standing could have talked the police around, but he hadn't even pushed it. Although she'd been relieved, she still had no real clue why he had gone.

"You came back," she accused.

"And you left."

"I had a buyer's trip." He'd made the mistake of calling to tell her he was in Rome on his way to see her. She'd left for the buyer's trip three days early.

"You were running, just as you ran the next time I attempted to see you."

"I owed my mother a visit."

"Your father told you I was coming to Rome. You knew that meant I was going to try to see you again. You took off on a flight for America less than an hour before I arrived."

"My father thought I might want to see you." A hollow laugh escaped her. Nothing could have been further from the truth, but Papa had done her a favor in warning her of Salvatore's intended travel plans.

"You ran away, Elisa, and I let you, but I cannot let you run any longer."

"I don't want to see you. That's not running away." Even he should be sensitive enough to realize she wanted to avoid a man who had cost her more than she had to give. "That is simply reality."

He flinched, or maybe it was a trick of the lighting. Old wiring sometimes made it flicker.

"It is also reality that your father has asked me to look after you. This I will do."

"I don't need looking after."

"You can say this?" There was no trick of the lighting now. Salvatore looked furious. "The security in this store is worse than I could have thought possible. The fact Signor di Adamo has not been robbed is by the grace of *il buon dio*. This store is the *amateur* thief's dream hit." His stress on the word "amateur" underscored his contempt for their security.

"There hasn't been money to make improvements in that area."

"That is no excuse. According to both Signor di Adamo and your father, you spend many days here alone. Is this true?"

Why was he asking her when they'd already said that it was?

"It's none of your business."

"You are my business."

That possessive statement set off something inside her. Pain that had been festering for months while she tried to pretend she was over him exploded in her chest. There had been no confrontation, no final end to their relationship. She'd walked out of the hospital against doctor's orders and refused to see Salvatore from that point on.

She shot to her feet without any thought of doing so and stormed forward until they were mere inches apart. Poking him right in his rock-solid wall of a chest with each word for emphasis, she said, *"I am nothing to you."* She managed to contain the level of her voice, barely. "I was nothing to you when you were screwing me, and now that we aren't even doing that I'm less than nothing to you. And you are nothing to me."

"You said I was the father of the child you lost."

She reeled from the words as if they'd been multiple body blows, staggering backwards, the pain so intense she did not know if she could contain it.

In a lightning-quick move that shocked her, he grabbed her wrist and pulled her the remaining inches while his mouth formed words she could not comprehend. Her body molded to his in a way that had once given her pleasure, but now filled her with loathing and fear. Loathing for her own physical reaction and fear that he would see it.

"Do not speak of yourself in this crude way. Whatever you were before, when we were together, you gave yourself to me. It was not ugly, as you make it out to be."

Whatever she'd been before? A virgin. That was what she'd been, but because the physical barrier had not survived her years in gymnastics he had assumed otherwise. Had in fact assumed she was the same sort of woman as her mother. A woman who flitted from one lover to another, Shawna had been uninterested in making a commitment to any of the long line of men parading through her life.

"I'm done giving myself to you. I've learned my lesson," she spat at him.

His jaw looked hewn from the hardest marble, his eyes glittered at her with fury.

She was glad. She wanted to make him angry, angry enough to leave her alone once and for all.

"We do not need to discuss this right now. I am here to see to your safety. Our relationship will wait."

"We don't..." She yanked herself away from him and stepped back toward her desk. "There is no relationship. None. Do you hear me? Leave me alone, Salvatore. You have no place in my life any more and you never will again."

He didn't say anything, just stared at her.

Then his gaze dropped below her neck and she wanted to scream. The whole time she'd been telling him off, the feminine parts of her body had been busy reacting to his scent, to the sensation of being held against him again.

"You're lying to yourself if you believe that."

She crossed her arms over the betraying rigid tips of her breasts and glared. "I'd rather go to bed with a sewer rat than with you, Signor Salvatore Rafael di Vitale."

His head jerked as if she'd hit him. She wished she had.

His next words totally shocked her because they were so calm. "Signor di Adamo needs several security upgrades before either you or he will be safe in the store, and, even with them, neither of you should be here alone at any time."

She fell back into her office chair, feeling the weight of her responsibilities too heavy to hold up any longer. Those upgrades, even the basic security measure of having two people in the store at all times, were not even pipe dreams. "I'm sure you're right, but nothing can be done."

"It must be done."

"There is no money."

Unmoved by that assertion, he said, "Nevertheless, it must be done."

Hadn't he heard her? Or was it that to a man like Salvatore, whose family owned one of the most prestigious and sought-after security firms in the world, the concept of not having any money did not compute?

He being richer even than her father, she supposed that was exactly the case.

"We can't." She sighed and rubbed her eyes with her thumb and forefinger, for a moment not caring if her enemy saw this sign of weakness. She was so tired. "Signor di Adamo is trying to hold on to the store for his grandson, but it gets harder every year."

"The auction for the crown jewels will bring in funds."

"Yes. A great deal of money that he needs very badly, but I don't know if even that will be enough. The security system isn't the only thing needing improvement around here."

She thought of the building's leaky plumbing and dodgy wiring. It was old, original to the store's inception. She shuddered to think of what sort of improvement Signor di Adamo's private apartments required.

"I will take care of it."

"He won't let you." One of the things that had drawn her to the old man was his fierce sense of independence so like her own. His pride would never accept charity.

She said so, but Salvatore just shrugged. Not really

a smile, the tiny tilt at the corner of his lips reminded her of things she would rather forget.

"I know how to work around a man's pride."

"I don't doubt it. You're good at manipulating people."

He shook his head. "I will not allow you to draw me into another argument, *cara*."

"I don't want to argue with you." It was true. The rage that had sprung up before was all but burned out. She just wanted him to be gone.

"This is good."

For a moment her mind could not comprehend what he had said until she realized she had only spoken aloud regarding not wanting to argue, not her desire for him to be gone. "I don't want to see you at all."

"We cannot have everything, *dolcezza*."

Dolcezza. Sweetness. He'd used to call her that because he said she tasted and acted so sweet. It scraped at wounds that were no longer raw and bleeding, but were not anywhere near healed. "Don't call me that."

"Where are the crown jewels now?" he asked, as if she'd never spoken.

"I told you. They're in the vault."

His body went taut, his attitude one of extreme alertness. "You've taken possession of them already?"

"Yes."

"Your father thought they were not being transported from Mukar for a week or more."

"That is what the former crown prince wished. He told everyone they were being transported just before the auction. He hoped to make the transfer in secret. It worked."

"Just because I did not know you had them does not mean no one is aware they have been brought here."

"They're safe in the vault," she repeated stubbornly.

"Perhaps, but you are not safe."

He kept harping on it and she knew he was right, but she didn't know what to do about it. And frankly, when she'd negotiated for the auction, she hadn't really cared about her safety one way or another.

The numbness after losing the baby and Salvatore had worn off, but a certain malaise of spirit lingered on. Sure personal happiness was out of her reach, she would risk anything, do anything to ensure it for a man who had been so good to her. Signor di Adamo.

Salvatore had moved without her realizing, while her mind had been off in its own little world. His hand brushed her cheek and she felt the gentle touch like a branding that both burned and physically hurt.

"I will never leave you alone."

Leaving her dazed from that small interchange, he spun on his heel and left her office.

CHAPTER TWO

SALVATORE waited for Elisa to come out of her office. She'd spent the remaining hours of the afternoon working on the auction while Salvatore and Signor di Adamo discussed new security features for the store and measures to keep both the old man and Elisa safe until the crown jewels were sold. Signor di Adamo handled customers as well, showing his grandson the ropes of the business, while Salvatore made phone calls on his mobile and ordered necessary equipment to be installed immediately.

It had been a pleasant afternoon, but the next few minutes did not promise to be so pleasant. He had to tell Elisa that he was going home with her. He had no choice, but he doubted very much she would see things that way.

She didn't.

Five minutes later she was glaring at him as if he had suggested something obscene. "No way." She shook her head so hard part of her hair slipped out of the French twist on the back of her head. It fell over one green eye and she impatiently shoved it aside. "You are not going home with me."

"If anyone knows of the jewels' whereabouts, neither you nor your employer will be safe. He will be staying with his daughter and son-in-law. You have no one."

An expression came into her eyes when he said

24

that, a bleakness of spirit he did not like and one he did not associate with the fiery woman who had been his lover. ''I don't have you either. Wouldn't have you. Even as a misguided gift from my father. You aren't going with me and that's final.''

With that she marched past him and out the door, leaving Signor di Adamo to lock up. Salvatore cursed and followed her.

''At least allow me to drive you home.'' He would take care of getting in the door of her apartment once they arrived.

''I'll catch the bus.'' And then she was running to do just that and Salvatore felt a wave of shock as he realized she'd thwarted him with less effort than it would have taken a five-year-old.

Furious, he rapped out orders to one of the men he'd brought in during the afternoon. He would see to Signor di Adamo and his grandson's safe journey home.

Salvatore slung himself behind the wheel of his black four-wheel drive and followed that damn city bus all the way to Elisa's apartment.

He was not in a good mood when he got there.

Elisa stepped off the bus and a very unpleasant word slipped past lips stiff with frustration.

Salvatore waited for her in front of her building with the look of a man ready to do violence. Only, if she knew anything about him, she knew he would not physically harm her. Even in the midst of his rage over the baby, he had kept his blows to the verbal variety.

All the same, she couldn't help the shiver of apprehension that skittered down her spine.

She approached the entrance warily, her eyes fixed on the spot of the red-painted door visible to the left of Salvatore's tall frame. If she could just get inside that door and away from the man in front of it, everything would be fine.

She stopped a foot away because he hadn't moved.

Nor had he spoken, but his body language spoke volumes and all of it bad.

"Do not ever run from me again."

She allowed herself to meet his gaze, pretending not to feel the shards of pain such a motion caused her deep inside. "Go take a hike. You don't dictate to me."

"Someone needs to. You have no concern for your own safety."

Her eyes widened at that. "What could possibly happen to me on the city bus?"

"If you don't know, you are more naïve than a woman of your age should be." Then he proceeded to spell out in graphic detail what could have happened to her, covering the range from a sex fiend accosting her to being kidnapped and forced to give her kidnappers the crown jewels.

When he was done, she fought both nausea and irritation.

"And if you think you are any safer in your apartment, you are a fool," he added when she remained silent.

"You're assuming other people know the jewels are at Adamo Jewelers, but there's nothing to indicate that is the case."

"Assume the worst and plan accordingly." He made no apologies for his cynicism and she hadn't expected him to.

Even when she'd loved him she'd recognized that he had a very pessimistic view of the world.

"Even if someone does know and wants to steal the jewels, the vault is on a timed lock mechanism," she said with satisfaction. "Signor di Adamo cannot open it before nine in the morning, no matter how much he might want to."

"That will not·prevent you from being used as a pawn in procurement of the jewels."

She sighed, knowing that in the most extreme scenario he could be right, but she was unwilling to believe the risk was all that great. "Please move." She dug for her door key in her purse. "I want to go inside."

"Have you heard nothing I have said?"

"I heard. I just don't believe." Aha. She'd found it. She withdrew the key and looked pointedly at the door behind him.

"Tough." Then in another one of those moves that always took her by surprise, he took her key. It was like the first time he'd kissed her. She hadn't been expecting that either.

She grabbed for the key ring, but he was already unlocking the door. Stepping back, he ushered her inside, her keys still firmly in his hand.

She stepped just over the threshold and then put her hand out. "Give it to me."

He ignored her outstretched hand and followed her inside, forcing her to move backward or be in the unenviable position of touching him again.

"It's a secured building, for goodness' sake."

"A locked entryway is not secure. Particularly one with a lock as old and easy to pick as that one."

The whole building was old and she liked it. Her apartment had character and the rent was cheap. She refused to live off of either of her parents, and Signor di Adamo could not afford to pay her what she was worth.

"Stop showing off your security-guard skills and give me back my key. I'm hungry and tired. I want to get to my apartment, make my dinner and go to bed."

"I am a security specialist, not a guard."

Not to mention being heir apparent to the whole company when his father decided to abdicate the throne.

"Whatever." She wasn't going to ask for the key again.

It was a good thing she didn't because it would have been wasting her breath. He started down the hall, his long-legged stride eating the distance to her apartment quickly.

When he stopped in front of her door, she looked at him askance. "How did you know my number?"

She had moved shortly after their breakup, unable to stand the memories the other apartment had elicited.

He rolled his dark brown eyes. "It's not that hard to find your address. In fact, give me fifteen seconds on a computer and I can find pretty much anyone's. However, in this case, I simply asked your father."

"Oh." She hadn't told her father about her brief affair and its disastrous end.

He would have gone ballistic and she had not been emotionally prepared to deal with any more at the time.

"You did not tell him about us," Salvatore said, mirroring her thoughts.

She shrugged and watched with a feeling of inevitability as he unlocked the apartment door with the other key on the ring.

"I didn't tell him about the baby either." She didn't know why she admitted that.

"Neither did I."

"I know."

Her father was ignorant of her pregnancy and miscarriage. Just as he was ignorant of what a rat his best friend's son really was. Her mother didn't know either. In fact, the only other person in the world who knew about the precious baby she had lost was this man. And she could hardly expect compassionate understanding from her worst enemy.

He pushed into her apartment and she had no choice but to follow.

"This is nice."

She looked around at the smallish apartment, which was almost a bedsit. It had its own bathroom, but the main area doubled as her daily living space and her bedroom when she pulled the ancient trundle bed down from the wall.

"It's bright, like you."

Like she used to be, maybe. She'd tried to make her home cheery and inviting with lots of yellow, white and rose-pink, but the décor had done little to improve her sense of loss and loneliness. Even the sunlight currently filtering through the window of the kitchenette seemed muted by the emotions that weighted her insides.

"Thank you," she replied stiffly to his compliment when the silence had stretched on.

He made an impatient sound. "Change your clothes and I'll take you to dinner."

"What is the matter with what I'm wearing?" she demanded, immediately on the defensive.

"Nothing. Let's go." He took her arm and the contact seared her just as she knew touching him again would do.

"I didn't say I was going with you," she said, trying to pull her arm from his grasp.

"Would you prefer to fix me dinner here?" He smiled as he'd used to and she felt a twinge in the region of her heart. "It has been a long time since you cooked for me, but I remember what a wonderful cook you are. I would enjoy the experience."

The sheer arrogance of that statement blew her away. "I would prefer you left." She glared up at him, carefully avoiding actual eye contact. "You've seen me safely home. There's no reason for us to prolong our time together."

"You seem to be under a misapprehension."

"What do you mean?" She gave up the struggle for possession of her arm. He wasn't letting go and every movement, even infinitesimal, increased her awareness of his closeness.

"I'm not leaving you alone."

Shards of fearful premonition sliced through her. "What exactly are you saying?"

"Until the auction is over, I am your faithful sidekick."

"You, faithful?" she scoffed, trying very hard to come to terms with his grimly delivered assurance.

The grip on her arm tightened. "I was never unfaithful to you."

She believed him, but she didn't want to. Not when he'd refused to believe her similar claim when she told him about the baby. She didn't want to give him the satisfaction of saying so, however. Instead she focused on the issue at hand.

"No."

His fingers uncurled from her arm and began a light caress. "No, what, *dolcezza?*"

"You are not staying with me." Her voice broke as his hand moved up to her collarbone. She felt like a bird being mesmerized by a snake. She couldn't move, but she knew to let him touch her was disastrous.

"I made a promise to your father. I will keep it."

"I don't need a bodyguard."

"That is not what he believes."

"My father does not dictate my life either."

"This is true. Unlike your sister, you have a disconcerting tendency to go your own way, but I would have thought that even so, your love for your father would not allow you to put him in a place of constantly worrying for your safety."

She wasn't going to be manipulated with that line. "According to him, he does that anyway."

"He had an episode with his heart last month. Did he tell you?"

She felt as if all the air had been sucked from the room. "No." Her voice came out a whisper. "He said nothing."

Why hadn't he called her? Why hadn't his wife, Therese, told her? As she thought it, she said it.

"I do not know, but perhaps he did not wish to worry you."

"I should have known!" The anguish she felt reminded her what an outsider she was. She belonged intimately to no one.

Salvatore studied her in a way that made her feel exposed. "Now you do. Are you willing to risk putting his heart under further stress?"

A sense of impotency filled her. Despite the fact they were not exactly close, she loved her father very much. And he *hadn't* looked well the last time she'd seen him. "No."

"Then I stay."

With a tremendous effort of will, she stepped back, away from that insidious touch. "No. If Papa is that worried, I'll agree to a bodyguard, but not you."

"It is too important an assignment for me to put it in the hands of another."

"Me, important?" She couldn't help deriding.

His jaw went taut and fire rained down on her from those dark chocolate eyes. "Keep pushing, Elisa."

His tone implied that, for her own sake, she had better do anything but. Only she couldn't make herself stop. There was too much pain inside her to govern everything that came out of her mouth when she was with him.

He'd hurt her and there was a terrible part of her that wanted to hurt him back, even if it was just with digs that did no more than annoy his sense of masculine pride.

"Get me a different bodyguard."

"That's not going to happen."

"I'll call Papa and tell him I don't want you around me."

"And will you tell him why?"

Salvatore's smooth question stopped her progress toward the phone on the small table beside the one armchair in her apartment.

"I don't have to tell him why."

"He wants the best for you and I'm the best. He will expect an explanation."

The problem was, she knew he was right. Even though several of the Vitale Security operatives were ex-military, none of them had been trained as thoroughly as Salvatore. His father and grandfather had seen to that, going so far as sending him to spend his formative years' schooling and training in an élite academy that taught a form of hand-to-hand combat second to none in the world.

It had been followed by a technical education at the university level that put him on a par with coordinators in the government's secret service.

"Then I shall tell him."

"And prompt a full-on heart attack? Does he mean so little to you?"

Her hands curled into fists at her sides. "Why are you doing this to me?" She spun to face him, her body vibrating with emotions she would give anything not to feel. "Haven't you hurt me enough?"

There it was. The truth laid bare between them. He had the power to hurt her and he had exercised it.

His face looked set in stone. "I am not doing this to hurt you. You need my protection."

"Just being around you hurts!" she cried, not able

to hide that from him any longer. Perhaps if she was honest, told him just how hard it was to be with him, he would withdraw from the fray and assign someone else to guard her. His Sicilian guilt should be good for something to her. "I can't stand the memories, Salvatore. Can't you see that? Not seeing you is the only way I can even begin to cope."

Pain shot through his expression, but then it was gone. "Pretending it did not happen is not coping."

Suddenly she knew. He wanted to force a confrontation. The man who found talking about his feelings right up there with Chinese water torture wanted to talk things out. She could see it in his eyes, in the stubborn set of his jaw.

She couldn't bear it. Rehashing the past would only hurt more, not heal.

He didn't realize that, of course. Because he was not hampered by the soul-destroying pain of a betrayed love. He had never felt anything more for her than sexual lust.

Desperate to avoid the confrontation she sensed was coming, she took the lesser of two evils. "You said you'd take me to dinner."

"We need to talk, Elisa."

She ignored that. "I'm really tired. I'd prefer not to cook tonight."

His frown expressed his irritation with her refusal to talk, but in the end, and to her undying shock, he nodded. "All right. If you do not need to change clothes, we can go."

"Just let me fix my hair and put on some lipstick."

Again he agreed, giving her a much needed re-

prieve from his presence as she closed herself into the
tiny cubicle that served as her bathroom.

Salvatore swore with frustration. He had believed it
would be difficult to overcome her aversion to him,
but had not been prepared for it to be almost impossible.

Elisa was not just angry with him. She hated him.

She had lost her baby because of him. She'd never
said so, but their final argument, the stress of that
confrontation had no doubt precipitated the miscarriage. It was a guilt he'd learned to live with, but he
would not live with the knowledge he had done nothing to make it right.

However, it was patently obvious she was not prepared for talk of marriage yet.

He had to woo her. His mouth twisted cynically.
He knew how he wanted to woo her. In bed. Seducing
her would be far easier than talking the stubborn
woman round to his way of seeing things. He would
enjoy it more too.

She might not like it, but her body still reacted to
him almost helplessly. Her pulse had increased with
the barest touch of his hand on her neck. Given
enough time and close proximity, it would simply be
a matter of *when* they made it back into each other's
arms.

No matter what had gone before, back in her bed
was a place he definitely wanted to be. Even marriage
was not too high a price to pay to know that all her
passion, all her fire would belong to him.

Elisa came out of the bathroom looking fragile, but
lovely. She'd brushed out her hair and pulled it back

with a clip. Her face had more color than it had earlier, but that was probably due to makeup rather than an improvement in her feelings. Not that her green eyes revealed anything. Their usually animated depths were blank of any emotion.

"Are you ready?" she asked, her voice as flat as her expression.

He detested that flatness, wanted to experience Elisa as she had been a year ago, not this buttoned-down stranger. But he had won one victory; he would consolidate his position before demanding more.

"I'm ready."

Just those two words and her eyelids flinched. He wanted to curse. He'd been a stupid bastard a year ago. Even if she was like her mother, as her father had said, she'd been different in one key way. She'd wanted to marry him when she discovered she was pregnant.

He still wasn't sure the baby was his. They'd only been together a month when she told him she was pregnant... What were the chances? But even so, he had decided to risk them because he had wanted her in his bed and in his life on a permanent basis. He'd made that decision too late and lived to regret his tardiness and stupidity.

"Let's go." He took her hand to lead her from the apartment.

She tried to pull away from him, the way she did from every single touch since they'd seen each other that morning in the jeweler's. And just as before, he didn't let go. She had to get used to his touch again. The prospect that she wouldn't was not a circumstance he wanted to contemplate.

"Where are we going?"

"Does it matter?"

"No."

"I did not think so."

Two hours later, they were back in the apartment, dinner having been nothing short of a disaster. She'd avoided looking at him, touching him and talking to him if she could.

The strain of it was showing on both of them.

She yawned.

"You need to go to bed."

She nodded.

He looked around the small apartment. The cozy and inviting undersized sofa didn't look so cozy as a possible bed. It was several feet too short for his over-six-foot frame. The pull-down bed would have been a slight improvement, but he had no doubt she would refuse to share it with him.

He looked at the floor with even less pleasure. "I suppose you'll expect me to bed down on the carpet."

Her eyes grew wide and a flush suffused her face. "I don't expect you to sleep here at all."

"I thought we settled this before we left." It was a blatant untruth. He'd known she would balk at him spending the night.

She stiffened in pure, independent female outrage. "You're not sleeping in my apartment."

"I am until the auction is over." His voice was as grim as his mood after dinner as the undesirable pariah. It was not an experience he was used to. Usually women fawned over him, even ex-girlfriends—but not this woman.

The look of horror that came over her made no improvement on his deteriorating mood.

"I'm not going to attack you," he ground out. "I'm here to protect you."

"It's impossible."

"Do you have a better solution? I'm not leaving you alone," he added before she could open her mouth to answer.

She gnawed at her lower lip in a gesture he remembered from before. It indicated she was in serious thought.

The look of horror turned to one of disgust. "If you insist on being my bodyguard, you can spring for a suite with two bedrooms at a hotel or sleep in the hall. You pick."

He stared at her. It couldn't be this easy. "A hotel."

"Fine. Give me a minute to pack."

Elisa threw clothes into a suitcase with little consideration for what she was packing. He'd looked shocked when she suggested the hotel, but she knew how intractable he could be. He would spend the night with her no matter what she wanted. Her apartment was out of the question. Just the thought of sharing such small living space with him made her cringe. She needed a door to shut between them, a room to call her own, a bed that would hold no memories.

Not that he'd ever shared her bed in this new apartment, but somehow, if he stayed, she knew it would feel tainted by his presence. She would have to move again.

She refused to consider why he had such a strong impact on her emotions still, or why hate sometimes felt like the other side of a bruised and bleeding love.

CHAPTER THREE

LYING in bed in the luxurious hotel suite later, memories she was too exhausted to fight washed over her.

Seeing him had brought it all back.

The debilitating pain. The sense of betrayal. The grief of loss, but also the glory of possession.

For a short while, it had been the most glorious time of her life. She had belonged to someone, had a place in his life. Not a grudging place as she had with her mother. Not an inconvenient place as she had with her father.

Salvatore had accepted and desired her for herself.

Or so she had believed.

If it were possible to go back in time she would go back, not to the point where she had met Salvatore in an effort to make a different choice with him. But she would go back to those four short weeks when she had believed herself loved as she loved, and if she could she would stay there forever.

She would never know the misery of his defection, the humiliation of his hurtful beliefs about her, the desolation of his lack of commitment to her. All of that would be in a future she would not have to live…if it could be so. Nor would she know the pain of losing the one being she had been certain to belong to forever, who she would have spent a lifetime giving a mother's love she had only ever dreamed of.

Her mind took her back to the moment when she had realized Salvatore was interested in *her*.

She'd been in Milan, attending an estate sale for a woman who was known for her jewelry collection. She remembered that her hotel room had felt stuffy because the air-conditioning unit was broken. The phone had rung just as she stepped out of a cooling shower. She'd considered letting the front desk just take a message, but in the end had traipsed across the room to pick it up, dripping and naked but for a thin towel wrapped around her.

"Hello?"

"Elisa. Salvatore here."

Salvatore? "My father's friend?" she squeaked, unable to believe he was calling her in her hotel room in Milan.

"I hope your friend as well, *cara*."

Oh, he was smooth. "Yes, of course. Is something the matter with him?"

"Him?"

"My f-father." She stumbled over the words, tongue-tied in a way she hadn't been since adolescence.

"Why should you think that?" his voice purred down the line at her.

"You're calling me."

"And a man cannot call a beautiful single woman with any other reason than to discuss her father?"

The gentle mockery had her knees going weak and she plopped down to sit on the edge of the bed. "Of course, I just…"

"Come, *cara*. Surely you realized I was interested in you."

Funnily enough, she hadn't. "You mean because you flirted with me?" she asked, feeling gauche for saying it. But still, "I thought you flirted with every woman."

"Do I?"

"I don't know." He was practically a stranger to her. She had grown up with her mother in America and, as close as her father and Salvatore's father were, she and Salvatore had met only infrequently over the years when she visited her father in Sicily.

"It seemed like it to me." He'd certainly flirted with her from the moment he found her on the sun-lounger by her father's pool her second day in Sicily the summer before.

She could still remember the smooth joke about mermaids and the sexy glint in his eyes. Italian men took female appreciation to whole new levels, but she'd found Sicilians in a class all by themselves. And Salvatore was the most impressive of the lot.

He had proceeded to flirt with her on and off over the next two weeks whenever he and his family were guests in her father's home or vice versa. Which, considering how close the two families were, was quite frequent.

She'd fallen for him like a ton of bricks.

It had never once occurred to her the feeling might be mutual.

"You will have to get to know me better," he was speaking again, "to see that I am not a flirt, *cara,* far from it."

"I will?" She liked the sound of that.

"*Sì.*"

"All right."

"I'll pick you up in forty minutes."

"What?" Now? He wanted her to get to know him now?

"For dinner."

"You want to have dinner with me?"

He made an impatient, but amused sound. "What do you think I am saying here?"

"That you want to have dinner with me?"

She might have been born to one of the most notorious and glamorous stars in Hollywood, but she lived a very quiet life and did not play man-woman games. She'd seen too much from a very early age and vowed never to be like her mother or the sycophants who populated Shawna's life. She would never cheapen intimacy as she'd seen it cheapened around her.

Only her lack of experience was making her sound like she was stupid. It would serve her right if he withdrew his dinner invitation, she thought in frustration.

"*Sì.* I want to have dinner with you and now you have thirty-five minutes in which to ready yourself."

He arrived thirty minutes later.

She was ready.

He took her to an elegant restaurant, where the food and the wine were delicious. They danced after dinner.

He pulled her into his arms, his hold intimate, and she did not complain.

It felt too good.

Sensations she had never experienced overwhelmed her as he swayed with her to the music.

It was sexual desire as she'd never believed it could be. Instantaneous. Hot. Unstoppable.

Pressing her even closer, he said, "You feel good, *dolcezza.*"

"So do you." Her voice was husky and low.

She'd never spoken that way in her life. It sounded sexy though.

"I am glad."

She tipped her head back to look at him and encountered eyes so intense, they burned right through her to the very core of her feminine sexuality.

"Sweet." His head lowered toward hers. "You are going to taste so sweet."

The kiss shattered every sense of who she believed herself to be.

She went up like a roman candle, burning with a heat she'd never even dreamed existed.

Unconscious of her surroundings, she twisted her hips against him, seeking some unnamable thing, some sort of relief from the conflagration of her senses. The caress only made it worse and he groaned, his lips taking on a hard sensuality that gave no quarter.

She desired none and responded with all the latent sensuality in her being.

Tearing his mouth from hers, he said, "We've got to get out of here, or I'm going to make love to you and get us both arrested for indecent exposure."

Shockingly she heard herself teasing him. "I've heard the police are quite understanding about that sort of thing."

He shook his head. "Do not joke. I am in agony. I want a bed with you on it. *Now.*"

Suddenly she realized where all this passionate intensity was heading and she froze. Literally. Stopping his rapid progress to the table.

He turned to her, his eyes black with desire, his mouth set in a grim line that she found slightly frightening. "What is it?"

"You expect to go to bed? Right now?"

His glare singed the edges of her heart. "What kind of game are you playing? If that kiss wasn't a prelude to bed, what the hell was it?"

She didn't play games, but he didn't know that. His accusation made her take quick stock, however. She couldn't very well tell him she'd never kissed like that in her life so had no experience of what it was a prelude to. Instinct told her that admitting her lack of experience to Salvatore would turn him right off. He was used to dating the most sophisticated sort of women.

"This is our first date."

"We did the mating dance for two solid weeks in Sicily. I would have taken you to bed then, but to do so while you were under your father's roof would have been disrespectful to your family."

"And you're so sure I would have gone?" Passion was fading, to be replaced by anger.

How dare he assume she would just fall into his bed like some—?

"Wishing would make it so," he said, interrupting her thoughts. "I wanted you, *cara*. I still do. Desperately. But if you are not ready, say it now. We will take it at your pace."

Sincerity was reflected in the tone of his voice, the

depths of his eyes, and she found herself falling right back under his spell.

"I want you too."

His nostrils flared and his body went even tenser, if possible. "Then let us go."

She nodded.

He took her to his home and it was then she learned that he lived a large portion of the year in Milan, overseeing his family's company satellite holding there.

Milan meant big business and big business meant ultra hi-tech security and superbly trained operatives.

He kissed her again when they got inside and she lost the battle before it had ever begun. She woke up hours later, her body aching in ways it had never done before with all her gymnastics routines. He slept on beside her, the sound of his breathing in the stillness a shocking reminder that she had never once shared another human being's bed.

Her hands stole to her cheeks. They felt hot in the darkness. She was blushing. No surprise that, not after what they'd done. He had thought she was experienced and the overwhelming passion he sparked in her had lent credence to that belief.

She edged out of the bed and tiptoed into the bathroom. She took a shower, washing a body that showed the signs of his loving. She closed her eyes against the evidence and finished cleansing herself. Stepping out of the shower, she saw herself in the full-length mirror opposite and went completely still.

The woman staring back at her was not the Elisa she had always known. This woman was a stranger. A sensual stranger. Her nipples were still hard and they ached slightly. There was a small mark on her breast. She remembered that kiss... He'd gone a little wild when she begged him to make the ache go away.

Those legs had wrapped themselves around a man with fierce urgency. Those hands had clung to his shoulders with all the strength of the supernatural, or so it had seemed. And that secret place between her thighs had experienced the most amazing pleasure she'd ever known, had welcomed him into her body with greedy need.

She felt different. As if she was connected to him on a spiritual level. Her emotions were engaged. Oh, yes, they were. She'd fallen in love so fast, she would doubt the reality of her feelings if they weren't so strong.

But what did he feel?

He did have experience. He'd been to bed with countless women, she would bet. Could tonight have meant anything to him the way it had to her?

She was terrified of going out there to find out that it didn't. Was he still asleep? He'd been sleeping soundly when she came into the bathroom. Maybe she should just get dressed and call a taxi, go back to her hotel. Avoid the whole morning-after awkward thing.

He'd said and done nothing to make her believe that the night was more than the temporary slaking of physical lust on his part. He couldn't love her as she loved him. Not a man so special and sexy.

He had women crawling all over him. A night of lovemaking that meant everything to her would mean nothing to him. She couldn't blame him. Despite years of avoiding casual sexual intimacy, she hadn't asked for any promises. He'd given none. He hadn't pretended to be in love, just in need.

Turning off the light before she opened the door, she let her eyes adjust to the darkness before stepping into the bedroom. She didn't want to wake him.

Her clothes were scattered all over. She headed toward a pile of white she guessed was her panties.

"*Cara*, I missed you. Come back to bed."

She stopped in the act of bending over to pick up that promising bit of fabric. "I... I think maybe I should go."

"No."

He moved so fast, she didn't see him coming, but between one breath and another he was out of the bed and beside her.

He swung her up into his arms. "You should stay."

"But..."

"But what, *cara*?"

The feel of his hair-roughened chest against her side was already impacting on her ability to think. "You... I..."

"*Si*. You and I. We are a couple and I do not like sleeping alone when my girlfriend is within reaching distance."

His *girlfriend*?

It had meant something to him, was her last coherent thought as his sensually demanding mouth settled over hers.

She was so happy over the next four weeks, she was sick with it. She spent a few extra days in Milan. He called her every night and several times a day for the next four days before showing up to stay a long weekend with her. She took personal leave and went back to Milan for a few days. He took her with him on one of his business trips to New York.

It was a magical time, right up until she started losing her breakfast.

She wasn't on the Pill, and the first time they made love he'd lost control and not remembered to use a condom. He'd never done so again and neither of them ever said anything about that single lapse, but it had consequences.

Consequences she frankly welcomed. The idea of having Salvatore's baby enthralled her.

She made a special dinner for him in her apartment the night she planned to tell him. He was flying in from Milan with the intent of spending two nights with her and she couldn't wait to see him again.

She had the door open before his hand could fall for the second knock.

His smile was lazy and tender. "You missed me, *dolcezza.*"

"Always."

He dropped his bag and pulled her into his arms, kissing her, and dinner was forgotten.

They were snuggling in bed much later, limbs entwined, when she told him.

"Salvatore…"

"*Sì.*" He was lazily rubbing her hip, his voice that deep, satisfied tone she'd come to associate with after making love.

"We've never discussed children."

His body tensed. "No, *dolcezza,* we have not."

She tipped her head back to look into his eyes. "You like them, don't you?"

His expression was unfathomable. "All Sicilian men like children."

She smiled. "That's nice."

"Is that all?"

"Not quite."

His hand stopped caressing her hip and his fingers pressed against her tightly, but he said nothing.

A little of the nerves she'd felt before his arrival came back to make her stomach flutter.

She settled her hand over it in an instinctive gesture. "I'm pregnant."

Nothing. No words. His expression did not change. His breathing changed though.

"Salvatore?"

"When did you find out?" His voice sounded harsh, as she'd never heard it before.

"This week."

A little of the tension in him drained away. "And you told me immediately."

"Yes. Of course. I wouldn't want to hide it from you."

"That is admirable." He didn't sound admiring, however.

"I know it's hard to come to grips with. I was pretty shocked myself."

His mouth twisted in a grimace. "I imagine you were."

"I mean I didn't know you could get pregnant with just one lapse…the first time. It wasn't even a good time in my cycle. It's almost a miracle when you think about it."

"A miracle?" He sounded as if he was choking.

"You are pregnant with another man's child and you call this a miracle?"

She sat up, shock reverberating through her. "What are you talking about? What other man?"

"Presumably whatever poor bastard was sharing your bed before you came to Milan."

"You think I got pregnant by another man?" she practically shrieked.

"Do not," he said so grimly that it scared her, "attempt to tell me this baby is mine."

"But it is." Her lungs didn't want to work and there was a pain in her chest as if she was being squeezed in a vice. "You forgot the condom that first time, don't you remember?"

He jumped out of the bed and stood towering over her, a fury unlike anything she'd ever seen glittering in his dark eyes. "And that was lucky for you, wasn't it? What's wrong?" He sliced the air with his hand. "Is the father of the baby not as rich as I am? Doesn't he want you any more?"

The taunts hurt. He'd never hurt her before and she'd come to believe he never would. Not like this.

"There is no other man." She tried to say it with conviction, but the words came out in a whisper. *"There's never been another man."*

His derisive laughter cut into her with the precision of a surgeon's laser. "You had sex with me on our first date... Your chances aren't good."

"Whose idea was that?"

"Don't play the innocent. In your circumstance, my impatience was like manna from heaven."

"I'm not playing at anything. I was a virgin!" She

hated having to say it like that, as if she was defending herself, which she was.

"Do not lie to me."

"I'm not lying."

"I am not taking responsibility for another man's mistake and you can take that assurance to the bank."

Both her arms crossed protectively over her stomach. "My baby is not a mistake!"

"Maybe not, but trying to convince me I am the father was. Who knows? I might have continued our affair and even helped you financially with the child if you had been honest." Scorn laced every word as he started throwing his clothes back on.

"What are you doing?"

His eyes derided her for asking such a stupid question. "I'm leaving."

She flew off the bed and across the room to him. It couldn't be falling apart like this. She refused to let a misunderstanding tear apart the framework of her happiness.

She grabbed his forearm, frantic to make him listen. "Please, Salvatore, darling. The baby is yours. I swear it. I love you. I wouldn't lie to you!"

He shook her off. "Stop this. You made your play. You lost. Accept it."

"It's not a play. I'm pregnant with your baby. Don't you *want* to be a father?"

His face contorted and then he spun away from her.

She stood, frozen by a reaction she had never expected as he finished dressing. She followed him when he walked out to the living room. His gaze flicked to the specially set table and his eyelid twitched, his mouth going more taut, but he said nothing.

He stopped at the door and then turned his head until they were once again making eye contact.

It hurt. Horribly. His eyes spoke volumes about what he thought of her and it was all terrible. "I will not tell your father about this. It would kill him, but don't try to convince him that baby is mine. I will not lie to protect you either."

From somewhere deep inside, defiance emerged. How dare he try to boss her around when he denied her and their baby? "I'll tell my father what I darned well please." She glared at Salvatore, her pain a ball of fire in her chest ready to explode and burn her heart to cinders. "You're the father and I won't lie to protect you either."

His lip curled in contempt. "Don't try it."

And the most painful realization she'd ever had burst upon her with the power of a nuclear explosion and with as much inner devastation. If he loved her anything like the way she loved him, he would believe her. Full stop.

"It was all just sex for you, wasn't it?"

"What else would it be with a woman like you?"

She didn't answer him. She couldn't. Her heart was breaking and it was a physical pain so debilitating, she could barely stand.

He turned and left and she stumbled to her bathroom to be sick over the toilet.

Salvatore sprawled on the suite's sofa, his long legs stretched out in front of him, and sipped at the single malt Scotch he'd poured shortly after Elisa had gone to bed. She had made a beeline for her room the minute they returned from dinner, saying she was tired.

This he did not doubt.

She looked more than tired, she looked breakable.

A year on from the tragedy, she was nowhere near being over it. One look into her beautiful green eyes told him as much. Sorrow lurked there. Grief. And all of it his fault. He'd been brutal with her and she'd lost the baby.

His fault.

He rubbed at his eyes. Would he ever forget the image of Elisa lying on her bed in a pool of blood?

She had tried to call him after that fateful night, the one in which she had attempted to convince him the baby she carried was his. He had denied her calls. She had come to see him in Milan and again he had refused to see her.

But gradually he had cooled down enough to think, to consider the possibility the baby was his, however unlikely. He realized he had allowed that other situation, the one born of youthful stupidity, to color his reaction to Elisa. So what if she was a lot like her mother, as her father claimed?

She was different with him. She never acted promiscuously with other men, had in fact behaved as if she was barely alive unless she was with him. If he had not been assured by her own father that she was the sophisticated replica of her mother, Salvatore would have thought she was innocent.

As innocent as she had claimed that awful night.

A month without her had severely dented the pride that had kept him away from her. He missed her like a physical ache and no amount of work made it go away. He had not even tried dating other women, feeling too raw from Elisa's betrayal.

Why had she tried to convince him the baby was his?

In the darkest hour of night, his conscience haunted him with the possibility that she had not been lying. Eventually he convinced himself that even if she was lying, he could understand why she had done it. She said she loved him and no doubt had been afraid of losing him.

Love wasn't something he thought about. It was an emotion women used to justify their passions and gave strong men an excuse to act weak. But even so, he could believe she cared about him enough to be afraid of losing him. Maybe she had even been afraid of facing pregnancy on her own.

Having made some decisions, he went to see her again.

She did not answer the door on the first knock, so he knocked louder. He knew she was home because he could hear her favorite singer faintly through the door. She never left electronic appliances turned on when she left the apartment.

He knocked a third time and then tried the door.

It turned in his hand. Angry with her lack of personal security, he shoved the door open and entered the apartment. He expected to find her in the bath, the only place he could imagine her being and not hearing his pounding. Only the door to the bathroom was open and the small room was dark.

He turned toward the bedroom, a feeling of unease assailing him. What if someone had broken in? What if she was hurt, or worse? Horrific images of all too real scenarios flashed through his mind, tearing at the moorings of years of discipline and teaching. He rushed into the bedroom, ready to do battle, but there was no foe.

Only the small lump made by a woman curled up beneath the covers.

She wasn't asleep, though. She was moaning and he could see tears streaking down her cheeks.

CHAPTER FOUR

"ELISA?" He fell to his knees beside the bed where she was facing.

Her eyes opened, the green depths dark with pain. "Salvatore? Why are you here?"

"Never mind. What is the matter?"

A sob snaked out of her of such anguish it hurt him to hear it.

"The baby. It think it's my baby."

He grabbed his cell phone and started dialing numbers. "I will call an ambulance."

She didn't answer, just moaned again and then cried out.

Ordering the ambulance took too long.

She was sobbing. "It hurts, *oh, God.*" She said it like a prayer, as if asking for divine deliverance.

She didn't get it because her body jerked and she shook her head, thrashing it from side to side on the pillow.

He put his hand over hers, which were locked together over her womb. "What happened?"

"I don't know." The words came out on another long wail. "I didn't do anything."

He tried to impart his strength to her through their hands, but he felt as if she was on another plane and he could not reach her. He could not prevent her pain. He could do nothing but mouth platitudes and hold her hands.

The emergency workers arrived. They worked around Salvatore at first, but then one of them asked him to move.

Suddenly Elisa, who acted as if she had not known the other men were in the room, grabbed Salvatore's hand with a desperately strong grip. "Don't let them move me. If they move me, I'll lose the baby."

"Elisa, you must let them take you to the hospital."

"No." Her fingers scrabbled against his. "If I stand up, my baby will die!"

"We won't make you stand," the emergency worker assured her, but she ignored him.

Her eyes were riveted to Salvatore's face. "Please, don't let me lose my baby. I promise…" Her voice trailed off as another contraction gripped her body, making her tense with pain.

"It is all right, Elisa. You must trust these men."

"I can't. They don't care." She was completely irrational and he did not know how to make her see. "It's my baby. Please, I can't let it die. I love it."

His own eyes burned and his throat was thick so he could not answer her right away.

Her eyes implored him. "Please, Salvatore. Don't let me lose my baby. I promise I'll never tell anyone who the father is. I'll move back to America. I won't bother you any more. Just don't let me lose my baby."

The words cut into him, each one a dull blade slicing at his conscience. "Do not say such things—"

The emergency worker who had not spoken pulled back the blanket and revealed a growing stain of red under Elisa.

Salvatore gasped. "Elisa…"

She'd looked down and then she'd screamed. The sound still echoed in his mind because it was a sound so full of torment it had gutted him, still gutted him every time he thought of it.

She had lost the baby before they left the apartment and had to be sedated to be moved. They had almost lost her from hemorrhaging.

She had ignored him when he went to see her the first few days out of the hospital. It had not mattered what he said, whether he kissed her or touched her. She'd pretended he was not there. He had gone on the fourth day, hoping she would be better, only to discover she had checked herself out.

She hadn't gone back to work, and with all his security training he still did not know where she spent the four weeks following her short stay in the hospital.

Elisa woke up to the sound of her own scream. Her heart was drumming against her chest, her body was clammy with sweat.

She reached for the lamp beside the bed and encountered hairy, male skin.

"*Cara,* are you all right?"

What was Salvatore doing in her bedroom? Then she remembered. Her new bodyguard. Until the auction was over.

"It was just a dream." She shook with the shocking cold the dream always brought with it. "No need for you to come tearing to my rescue."

"It sounded more like a nightmare." His voice reflected not even a whisper of irritation with her short temper. "Were you dreaming about the baby?"

"Yes. What made you ask?" Surely he could not know about the dreams that haunted her.

"You screamed the same way you did when you realized you had lost it."

"I didn't know nightmare screams came with tonal indicators to tell you what event they harked back to."

"This is not a cry I am ever likely to forget."

Her breath shuddered out of her along with any defiance. She hated the aftermath of the dream almost as much as the nightmare itself. "Me neither."

"I am sorry."

She didn't ask what for. She didn't need to. He'd told her in the hospital. He blamed himself for her losing her baby. If he had ever at any point have said *their* baby, she might have forgiven him.

"Me too." Then because she so desperately wanted him to stay, she asked him to leave. "I'll be fine. You can go back to your room now."

He got up and left without another word. Feeling bereft and knowing she had no right to, she huddled under the covers, trying to rid herself of leftover feelings from her nightmare.

A few minutes later, he was back. He left the door open to the suite's living area, where he had turned on some lights. Reflected light spilled through the opening, dispelling some of the dark shadows in her room.

He stopped beside her and handed her a hot mug. She sipped at it and almost choked on the strong spirits.

"It is warmed brandy. It will help you sleep."

She nodded her thanks, unable to talk, and drank the brandy.

"Do you have these nightmares often?"

Only for the first month after she had lost the baby. "No, but last night I remembered."

"I also."

That brought her head up to look at him, but his expression was shrouded in the darkness. "It wasn't your fault."

"Was it not?" He turned and went to the window, drawing back the drape, and looked out into the blackness beyond. "The doctor told me that emotional stress can cause miscarriage and you were definitely under emotional stress because of me."

She couldn't deny that, but neither could she blame him for something that was no one's fault. She blamed him for not believing her, for accusing her of trying to trick him and for rejecting their child, but she did not hold him accountable for the death of their baby. "Maybe it was for the best."

He spun back to face her. "What?"

"I know what it is like to grow up an accidental baby, unwanted." She'd thought about it a lot and as much as she had wanted her baby, she could not ignore the problems inherent in the life of a child rejected by its father before birth.

"But you wanted this baby." His voice was thick, almost as if he was holding back some intolerable emotion.

"Yes, but you didn't. She would have grown up wondering what was wrong with her that she wasn't worthy of her father's love. I'm not saying this to make you feel guilty, but so you understand that sometimes tragedies like this happen for a reason.''

"I would have wanted my child.''

Only he hadn't believed the baby had been his. She didn't labor the point. The brandy was having its effect, and right now she just did not want to fight with him any more.

He didn't give her the chance. "Did you feel unloved by your father?''

She sighed, trying to untangle the mess of emotions she had felt about her father during her growing-up years. "No. Not unloved, but not particularly wanted either. I was the symbol of his one big mistake. I wasn't the kind of daughter he could understand, not like Annemarie. I was different, not traditional, not really Sicilian. I didn't fit and I felt that. Every summer I came to stay and reminded him that his perfect little family had a cuckoo in it.''

Salvatore sat down on the bed. "This hurt you.''

What was the use in denying it? "Yes.''

"And your mother?''

"She hated the very word mother, but she was too independent and proud to let Salvatore have custody of me. So, I spent a lot of time in boarding-school or with nannies.''

"That is terrible.''

She shrugged. "It was all right really. I hated living at home.''

"Why?''

"My mother surrounds herself with sycophants and neither she nor they have any concept of commitment and caring in a relationship. It was ugly and it hurt to see my own mother hopping from one man's bed to another so easily.''

Salvatore wanted to ask why, if that was true, she had allowed herself to become like her mother, but he didn't. She was talking to him more freely than she had since telling him about the baby.

''So, when you were an adult, you settled in Italy, away from your mother.''

''Yes.''

''But also away from your father. Why didn't you move to Sicily?''

''Papa is a traditional Sicilian father. If I lived near him, it would have to be with him and that would not be fair to either Therese or Annemarie.''

''What do you mean?''

''I would not want to disrupt their home life like that. They tolerate my visits in the summer. That's enough.''

''They are your family.''

''No.'' Resignation, not sadness, laced her voice. ''I don't belong.''

He felt as if he'd been kicked by a horse in the solar plexus. This woman, who had enough confidence to practically run Signor Adamo's business single-handedly, did not believe she had a place in her own family.

That knowledge was still haunting Salvatore the next day when he drove Elisa to work.

She was quiet, subdued, but the hostility that had marked her reaction to him the day before was missing and for that he was grateful.

''Have you sent the invitations to the auction?'' he

asked her as he parked the car in front of Adamo Jewelers.

"Yes. Several people have already replied. It should be a good turn-out."

"I'll need a copy of the guest list and those who have agreed to attend."

"All right."

"You have stopped fighting me."

She opened her door before he had a chance to come around and do so. "What's the point? The auction is in less than two weeks. When it's over, you'll be gone."

She slid out of the car and did not hear his muttered, "Do not bet on it."

Several hours later, Elisa seriously questioned her assumption that there was no point in arguing with Salvatore. She had thought that her best defense against the feelings he engendered lay in ignoring him. It hadn't worked. She felt as if her life had been taken over by a steamroller and she was getting flattened in the process.

She and Salvatore were alone in the shop. It was close to closing time and Signor di Adamo had already left. So had Salvatore's men who were installing the new security system. It was not finished. They'd run into a snafu with the old wiring and it would be tomorrow before it could be fixed.

Salvatore had been furious, but there had been nothing anyone could do.

Which had given her a perverse, if silent, satisfaction. He could not order the entire universe to suit his pleasure, no matter how much he might like to or what kind of kick he got out of bossing her around.

Keeping to her plan of least resistance, therefore least interaction with him, she had ignored, or at least pretended to ignore, his constant presence. When he and Signor di Adamo discussed her as if she were not there, she acted as if that were the case. She refused to be drawn into his discussions with Signor di Adamo regarding security measures.

She had kept her mouth shut when he dictated that he and she would stay behind to close the store. Alone. She had pretended not to notice him making reservations for dinner that night for the two of them at a restaurant they had frequented during their brief affair. Even though he'd made them right in front of her.

But this latest was just too much. She smacked the hand away that was offering her the small golden rose pin and glared up at him. "I am not wearing a tracking device."

Salvatore's brows rose, but his mouth curved in satisfaction. "I thought you did not want to argue with me."

She felt like a tea kettle ready to boil over. "I don't want to be with you at all. I thought if I didn't argue with you, I could ignore you, but you're determined to make that impossible, aren't you?"

His dark brown eyes narrowed and his mouth set grimly. "Yes."

That stopped her in the process of turning around and walking away. She spun back to face him, frustration making her so tense her muscles ached. "Why, Salvatore? Why torment me?"

"I have no desire to torment you. You belong to me. I will not allow you to pretend I do not exist in your life."

She did not believe he had just said that. "You cannot be real. *No way did you say that.*"

"I said it. Accept it."

"I don't belong to you." The very idea was obscene. "You rejected our child and now you want to lay claim to me." No way. Not in a thousand years.

She hardly realized she'd been saying the words out loud until he responded.

"I did not reject our child."

"How do you work that one out?" she asked, her voice ridiculing him. "Oh, I've got it." Then she touched her finger to her temple and pursed her lips, nodding. "You didn't believe the baby was yours, therefore you did not reject your own child. How convenient for you."

She hated the bitterness in her voice, but he had lanced the wound and now all the poison seemed to be flowing out of it regardless of what she wanted.

"You tell me you are pregnant when we have been together four short weeks and what do you expect me to believe? *Porca miseria!* Do you believe I wanted to think of your body welcoming the seed of another man?"

"If you found it so painful, why think it, then?" She'd done nothing to make him believe such a thing about her. "Admit it, Salvatore, I meant nothing to you and you didn't *want* to believe the baby was yours."

"You do not know what I wanted!"

She stepped back at the volume of his voice. He

was a passionate man, but he'd never yelled at her, even that awful night when he rejected her and the baby. "I'm sorry but I do. Your actions speak for themselves. You had no reason to believe I slept around and yet you made that assumption because *you wanted to,*" she repeated.

"Your own father told me you were like your mother," he said, his voice so accusing she cringed. "That is right." He nodded as if her reaction was his due. "Francesco Guiliano, a Sicilian man that would never make up tales about his own daughter. *He* said you were like Shawna Tyler, famous actress even more legendary for her numerous love affairs than her beautiful face or acting ability."

There had been nothing of love in her mother's frequent liaisons, but Elisa didn't speak that truth aloud. She was reeling like a drunk on a Saturday night from Salvatore's claim her father had said those things about her.

"Papa told you I'm like Shawna?" *That hurt.* It hurt so much, she almost doubled over with the pain of it.

They weren't close, but she thought her father knew her better than that. She thought he understood how much she had hated her mother's lifestyle. She'd never actually told her father so. Somehow saying it out loud had always felt like a disloyalty to her mother, but when had she ever done anything to justify his belief that she indulged in casual affairs?

He would never think such a thing about Annemarie. His perfect, traditional Sicilian daughter.

Salvatore was watching her, with an expression almost like compassion. On top of everything, it was just too much.

"Don't pity me! Papa is as wrong as you were, but I don't care, do you hear me? I don't care," she said, uttering the lie with more desperation than conviction.

She was a grown woman. She did not need her father's good opinion any more than she needed Salvatore's. If the only two men in her life she had ever loved wanted to think she was some kind of slut, let them.

Salvatore opened his mouth to speak, but then shut it again with a snap. His head swiveled and he focused on something in the street outside the shop.

She started to say something, but he shook his head and put his forefinger to his lips.

Cocking his head slightly, he took a gliding step toward Signor di Adamo's apartment.

Her gaze skittered to the door. It was slightly open and she couldn't remember if it had been left ajar when her boss took his leave. Shivers of apprehension shook her as all of Salvatore's warnings replayed through her mind.

She should have moved the inventory to the vault over twenty minutes ago, but her argument with Salvatore had kept them in the store past closing time and she'd done none of her usual closing routines.

The door to her boss's apartment slammed open. Salvatore leapt toward it. In that same moment, two men wearing grotesque carnival-style masks came bursting through the front door.

The deadly-looking gun in the hands of the man coming in through the back entrance was more terrifying than the hideous images on the masks of the other men.

In a blur of movement, Salvatore landed a kick against the one with the gun, sending him back through the doorway.

The other men rushed him and he shouted at her, "Get in the vault, and shut it."

She ran for the vault, but she wasn't shutting that big steel door with Salvatore on the outside.

He managed to send both men to the floor, stunning them. She could see through the crack of the door to Signor di Adamo's apartment though and the gunman was already getting up. Another black shape moved and she realized the gunman was not alone.

"Salvatore!"

He heard her scream and spun around.

She waved frantically at him. "There are more! Come on."

"I can handle it. Close the door, *cara*. Now."

"No. Not without you."

Salvatore swore.

His eyes flicked to the men on the floor. One of them started moving.

Frantic with fear for his safety, she screamed, "Salvatore, come on!" Then, instinctively knowing he would not put her at risk, she repeated her earlier warning. "I'm not shutting this door with you on the outside!" She took a step outside the vault to prove to him she meant what she said.

He said a word she'd never heard him use, even in the throes of passion. Then he kicked the door to the apartment with one powerful thrust of his leg, sending the men behind it staggering into each other. Almost simultaneously, he spun on his heel and ran toward her.

Shoving her completely into the vault, but remaining on the outside, he went to shut the door. She cried out in rejection of that move and grabbed his arm, her grip so tight he'd have to hurt her to break the hold.

Gunshots sounded and the wall beside the vault exploded in a shower of plaster and splintered wood.

Cursing again, he pushed inside the vault and, yanking the heavy door shut, he immediately spun the locking mechanism into place. The sound of heavy bolts shifting was accompanied by more gunfire, but none of the bullets penetrated the one-foot-thick door to the vault.

Soon, even the sound of the gunshots faded as the door sealed completely. She pressed the button for the emergency light and was relieved when the low-level glow penetrated the absolute darkness of the vault.

Salvatore yanked out his cell phone and swore. "No signal."

"It's a thick vault, but someone will have heard the gunshots and called the police." More than one person no doubt. Gunshots were not the usual evening sounds in the small town.

"Sì." He turned to her, his eyes accusing. "Damn it, Elisa, why did you disobey me?"

Typical arrogant, macho male. "Even you aren't impervious to a bullet, Salvatore. They could have killed you." Just the thought had her teeth chattering in shock. "Why didn't you come to the vault immediately?" Tears clogged her throat and burned her eyes. *"You could have been shot."*

His expression was unreadable. "And this would have bothered you?"

How could he ask such a stupid question? "Ye-es." Her voice broke and the word ended up a terror-filled wail.

He shook his head and pulled her into his arms with tender savagery. "I am fine. This is what I am trained to do, no?"

"You m-mean y-you risk your life like th-this all the time?" she stuttered out past the tears. It was an aspect of his business that had never sunk in before, disturbing her when it should not matter at all.

She knew what he was, but to her he had always been the suave tycoon, not the dangerous security expert that could send three men flying in seconds.

"I own the company, *amore*."

"But you're trained for this." Her voice ached with accusation and fear of what that meant.

He smiled cynically. "It is a rare thing for me to act as a bodyguard."

She gripped the lapels of his suit jacket. "How rare?"

"This is the first time."

"So, as a favor to your father's best friend, you put your life at risk." How stupid. "You could have let another man guard me...a regular bodyguard." Someone used to risking his life for the client, someone who was not the man she had once loved.

He tucked her against his body, her head fitting perfectly into the hollow below his chin. "I would have allowed no other man to protect you."

And she even understood why. "Because you feel guilty."

"And should I not feel this?"

The confirmation acted like freezing water poured over the small spark of hope that had begun to ignite inside her that he felt something real for her after all.

She didn't want his guilt. She had tried to convince herself she didn't want *anything* from him in the way of emotion, but the stress of being shot at, having him shot at, realizing that they both could have been killed, all of it came together to decimate her defenses.

His hands moved on her back, soothing her, pressing her into his body.

And what she felt then scandalized her. "You're turned on!"

"It has been a long time for me. Having you near…" He shrugged. "Besides, it has been long known that danger is an aphrodisiac. Ignore it, and I will manfully try to do so as well."

She tilted her head back and looked into eyes that burned black in the dim light. "That would be a first." She meant to say it lightly, in an attempt to relieve some of the pressure building between them, but her words came out husky and inviting.

His nostrils flared and his jaw clenched. "This is very true. I do not resist you well, *cara*."

She didn't say anything. She couldn't. Her body was responding to him just as it used to. Her breasts ached for his touch. Of their own volition, her legs separated slightly.

He groaned. "You do not make it easy."

"What?" She couldn't think what they were talking about. A fire of need was whooshing through her body, leaving sensitized nerve endings and painful longings in its wake.

He muttered something and lowered his head, his lips covering hers with blatant passion and possession.

CHAPTER FIVE

SHE had no thought of refusing him.

Not in that moment when the past did not matter. Too much had happened in the present. Later it would all matter again, but not now.

Her mouth parted and he took immediate advantage, deepening the kiss, sliding his tongue against hers. Tasting her, letting her taste him.

Her body arched toward him.

It had been so long.

Hands curling around his neck, she reveled in the intimacy of his kiss…his touch.

He cupped her bottom, kneading her flesh and letting his fingers slide dangerously close to the apex of her thighs.

She moaned.

"*Sì, amorino*. That is right." His lips moved against hers in affirmation, exciting her even more as his breath teased her lips. The kiss grew voracious, desires long denied exploding between them with the power of a pyrotechnic display.

She sucked his bottom lip into her mouth and bit lightly.

Suddenly she was being lifted and they were moving. He stopped when she was against the cold metal wall of the vault. The fact that she could feel the chill on the backs of her thighs only registered in her periphery. He'd pulled her skirt up and left her bottom half exposed to his wandering hands, but she didn't care.

All she wanted was to feel his skin against hers. She scrabbled for the buttons on his shirt, undoing them with more haste than finesse. Her dress came off and they were flesh to flesh with her breasts nestled into the fine curls of hair on his chest.

"I want you, *dolcezza.*"

She didn't answer. She couldn't—his lips were pressed against hers with passionate intensity—but she wanted him too.

Then he was kissing her neck. "Sweet, so sweet..."

And for no reason she could fathom, those words, words he had spoken so many times when they had made love before, woke other memories. Pain she had thought anesthetized for this brief span of time sliced through her, annihilating her ardor and leaving her trembling with dark emotions, not desire.

Her head fell back against the wall, her hands immobile against him. "I'm so sweet you thought I tried to land you with another man's child."

"Do not think of this now." He sounded desperate.

No doubt he was. Salvatore was more than a little oversexed and there was no denying he wanted her. Not with the bulge of his erection pressing so hard against her stomach.

"I can't stop thinking of it," she whispered, her own despair trimming her voice to almost nothing.

His groan was primal man deprived of his mate. "Not now, Elisa. Let us speak of this later."

"We don't have a later."

He went completely still. The silence screamed be-

tween them. He stepped back, letting her stand on her
own, and dropped his hands away from her. "You
are wrong about this. We have a past. We have a
present." He emphasized each point with one hand
slicing down toward the other. "And the future will
see us together as well."

"I won't have another affair with you." Even he
had to have more sensitivity than that.

"I want you for my wife."

One year ago those words would have thrilled her
to bits. Now they were more like backhanded blows
than the declaration she had once longed for.

"So only marriage will assuage your Sicilian
guilt." She shook her head hard enough to make her
dizzy. "Forget it."

He would have to find his personal absolution
someplace else. It would not happen in marriage to
her.

"You wanted to marry me once."

"I didn't—"

His hand covered her mouth, the touch gentle despite the tension vibrating off of him. "Do not lie.
You wanted this, or you would not have told me
about the baby, no?"

"A man deserves to know when he is going to
become a father."

"And what did you expect?" His hand slid down
to cup her neck. "You expected me to do the honorable thing, to offer marriage. Why not? We were
already lovers. Our families are close. What could be
more natural?"

Having him repeat all the beliefs that had once

gone through her head added another subtle element to the mixture of sorrow inside of her.

"That was then. This is now."

He sighed and stooped down to retrieve her shift dress from the floor. "Here, put this on." His eyes went over her like two hands. "If you do not, we will both probably regret the consequences."

She took the pile of rust-brown fabric with a trembling hand and then slipped it over her head. Once she had it on, she did not feel appreciably less vulnerable.

The ease with which he had taken it off haunted her.

How could she want this man who had hurt her so much?

What was she, some kind of masochist?

He shrugged off his jacket and left his shirt unbuttoned. He hadn't been wearing a tie.

While fresh air piped into the vault in case of just such an emergency, the air-conditioning was minimal. It was not stifling, but it was not comfortably cool either and there was some justification for him leaving the shirt undone. That did not make it any easier for her to deal with all that sexy male muscle on display.

Ignoring him and his half-naked appearance, she staggered to the back of the vault. Her legs were still shaky from her close brush with death and lovemaking.

She stepped into a commode the size of an airplane bathroom that had been walled off in one corner of the vault, complete with a bi-fold door for privacy. Pushing the door closed, she leaned against it. After several deep breaths she leaned over the tiny sink and splashed cold water onto her face.

There was no mirror, but she could feel her hair falling down around her face. She pulled out the combs holding it in a now lopsided bun and finger-combed it. She left it down, knowing there was no chance she could get it back into a tidy up-do without a mirror or comb.

Taking a deep breath, she pulled the bi-fold open.

He was standing just on the other side.

Waiting.

She sidestepped him. "It's free if you need it."

"When I was eighteen years old, I had a girl-friend."

"That's not exactly breaking news, Salvatore. Women flock to you like bees to honey."

He didn't respond to her sarcastic jibe. "Her name was Sofia Pennini. She was beautiful. She was sexy and she was experienced. She was also four years older than I was."

His opening up like this so shocked her that she found herself stopping in front of him and listening with more attention than she'd been willing to give him in a year.

Muscles in his jaw corded with tension. "She se-duced me the second time we went out."

Elisa's snort of disbelief came as no surprise to Salvatore. In *their* relationship, he had done all the seducing.

He shrugged in acknowledgement of her skepti-cism. "I had spent my teenage years surrounded by males. The training I received was accompanied by an austere life that did not include exposure to a woman's sophisticated wiles.''

"You've certainly made up for it since then.''

"I can do without the commentary. I am trying to tell you something.'' And he did not like sharing this memory with her. It made him a fool, but she deserved to know the truth. "When I met Sofia I thought I knew the score, but the truth was I was a babe in arms compared to her. She knocked me sideways with lust. I could not get enough of her.''

Elisa huffed out a breath and glared at him. "I'm supposed to *want* to hear this?''

This evidence of jealousy gave him a small seed of hope. "It is important, for what I experienced with her had a great deal to do with how I reacted to you last year.''

Sexy lips firmed in a grim line, she nodded. "Go on.''

"We had been sleeping together for about six weeks when she told me she was pregnant with my baby.''

"I bet you believed *her.*''

He refused to be baited by the sarcasm. "I did.''

Elisa's mouth dropped open and then it snapped shut and her eyes shot messages of murder and mayhem at him. "I guess her father never told you she was a tramp.''

"Your father did not call you such a name.'' He deeply regretted telling Elisa what her father had said at all. It had hurt her and that only added more weight to the guilt he carried regarding her.

"Whatever. You were telling me about this pannini person.''

"Not pannini, Pennini." He felt his lips curve at her sarcastic wit. "She is not a loaf of bread, *cara.*"

"She's not your ex-wife either. You've never been married."

Remembered humiliation made him frown. "No. She is not my ex-wife. I planned to marry her though."

"Lucky her."

He shrugged, feeling uncomfortable all of a sudden. "She thought so. My family is rich. I am my father's only heir. Already I was being groomed to take over the business."

"What are you saying, that she tricked you?" Again Elisa sounded disbelieving. "I suppose that baby wasn't yours either."

"Exactly."

Suspicion narrowed her eyes. "Are you sure?"

"Sì. Very sure. My father, he was furious when I told him I intended to marry this girl. He threatened to cut me off, but I did not care."

"He didn't want you to marry the mother of your baby? That doesn't sound very Sicilian."

"He did not believe the baby was mine."

"So it's hereditary."

He wanted to touch her so badly, to once again kiss her and wipe that look of distrust and antipathy off her face, but he knew she would not accept it. "My father was right."

Elisa's arms crossed under her very lovely breasts. "Sure he was."

"He investigated her and discovered she had been sleeping with another man, who happened to be ten years her senior and married, only a week before she and I became lovers.''

''That doesn't mean the baby wasn't yours.''

Too tense to remain motionless, he paced to the other side of the vault. ''No, it does not, but the blood tests done during her pregnancy did.''

''Blood tests?'' Her voice sounded close and he turned.

She was standing right behind him, having followed him the few feet across the vault.

''She had to have an amniocentesis. I do not even know why, but my father got hold of the results. The baby's blood type was neither hers nor mine.''

''And he told you.''

''On the night before I planned to elope with her and marry against my father's advice.''

''What did she do when you confronted her?''

Elisa knew him well. ''She cried. She was desperate. The father refused to leave his wife for her. Sofia's family were angry and threatening to disown her.''

''She must have been terrified.'' The sound of compassion in Elisa's voice reminded him how gentle her heart was.

''Yes.''

''What did you do?''

''I gave her money to begin life over somewhere else.'' He had been unable to just walk away.

''What happened to her?'' She rolled her eyes when he didn't answer. ''Come on. I know you didn't just dump her like that.''

''I dumped you.'' It was a shameful truth he would have to live with for the rest of his life.

Even the dim light could not disguise the fact that her face drained of color, but she didn't back down. "We're not talking about me. We're talking about her and your eighteen-year-old self."

"She married a year after the baby was born."

"A happy ending for her."

"But not for me." Because the experience had left him distrustful and that distrust had cost both him and Elisa dearly.

"Did you love her?"

"I wanted her."

"As you wanted me."

He did not like hearing her compare their relationship to the one he had had with Sofia. "It is not the same."

"Right. You trusted her more than you trusted me."

"My lack of trust in you was *because of her*." Frustration made his voice biting when what he wanted to do was soothe the look of hurt from those beautiful green eyes.

"And there was the fact my father told you I was like Shawna."

"*Sì.*" Something he never should have told her.

Elisa's head and heart were reeling. A year ago she had paid the price for another woman's sin and Salvatore's lacerated male pride.

It made sense of so much she had not understood. Inconsistencies that had haunted her and made her wonder what she had done wrong to make him distrust her so much.

She'd had two strikes against her and hadn't even

known it. Her own father had talked her down to
Salvatore. That was not a truth she was ready to deal
with on top of everything else and yet she had no
option but to do so. Papa thought she was like
Shawna despite the fact that she'd never done anything to make him think it.

Had she?

Second-guessing a past she knew was blameless,
even if others did not, was a useless exercise she refused to get into.

Then there was the fact she had got pregnant too
fast for Salvatore to believe the baby was his...
because of what he had gone through with Sofia.

She flicked him a glance that encompassed his
whole person, but denied eye contact. She could not
handle that right now.

"Thank you for telling me." Having had all she
could take of emotional drama for the time being, she
was ready to focus on the more prosaic. "We're going to be in here all night; we might as well get settled."

Turning away from his silent, watchful figure, she
walked back to the corner with the lavatory and the
emergency stash of food stored in the small cabinet
on the other side of the bathroom's back wall.

Like many jewelers, Signor di Adamo had
equipped the vault in case there ever was a robbery
and he or another employee was forced to take refuge
in it. The timed locking mechanism meant that huge
metal door would not open before nine the following
morning. Her boss did not have an override code and
the vault was so old she doubted the security company that had installed it still had the code on record.

Even if they had, it would take a burning building for them to agree to use it.

It was a security precaution meant to protect the owner from being forced from his bed by would-be thieves and intimidated into opening the vault. Only this time it was useless. Because of her argument with Salvatore, she hadn't gotten the stock moved into the vault.

"Poor Signor di Adamo. Those men probably stole all the jewelry before leaving the store. He is insured, but this might be enough to make him give the store up." And that would be sad after all she and the old man had sacrificed to keep the business going.

"They were after the *crown jewels,* not the modest collection in the storefront. Once they realized the jewels were locked safely in the vault, I doubt they took the time to clear the cases before running."

"At least the crown jewels are safe. We can still have the auction. There is a chance Signor di Adamo can save the store."

They had not been taken out of their storage drawer in the vault since their arrival.

"For now."

She looked up from rummaging in the cupboard for foodstuffs that might make an adequate dinner for the two of them. "Why do you say that? Surely they won't risk coming back now that the police will know to be looking for them?"

He reached out and brushed her cheek, a small smile playing at the corner of his mouth. "You are innocent in many ways."

She jerked back from the touch. It was an involuntary movement, but it made him frown. Tough.

"Just not the ones that count." The words tumbled out before she thought and she regretted them. Not because she didn't think he deserved the dig, but because she did not want to re-open that conversation. "Forget I said that."

"It is forgotten." The grim set of his mouth said differently, but she wasn't about to take issue with him over it.

"Elisa, *piccola*. Are you in there?"

The sound of Signor di Adamo's voice echoing in the small enclosure shocked her, and for a minute she could not quite figure out what was going on.

Not so Salvatore. He was on the other side of the vault in a flash and speaking into the small black box recessed in the thick metal wall near the door. "This is Salvatore. Elisa is with me."

"Are either of you hurt?" Signor di Adamo's voice sounded strained, older than his sixty-two years.

"No. Can you open the vault?"

"The security company that installed it went out of business two years ago."

That was news to her. Had she known, she would have tried to get her boss to do something about transferring the override information to another company.

Salvatore swore. "This means you have no way of overriding the timed lock, no?"

"This is the truth. Praise the good God that you are both all right."

Salvatore said something succinct, but did not press the communication button, so Signor di Adamo did not hear.

They discussed the details of the break-in and how she and Salvatore had ended up locked in the vault.

Her boss's exclamations were replaced by the cool authority voiced by the local police. They took Salvatore's statement via the intercom box while Elisa chewed on her lower lip in worry.

"Ask them about the inventory," Elisa told Salvatore.

Salvatore pressed the button. "Elisa wishes to speak to Signor di Adamo."

He moved out of the way, allowing her to ask for herself.

She pressed the button and spoke into the small box, all the while hoping Salvatore had been right. "Signor di Adamo, I did not have the opportunity to put the trays in the vault before the break-in."

"I noticed this." His voice was quizzical, but not unduly worried.

"So, they, um…didn't take anything?" She'd been derelict in her duty to her boss and would be devastated to discover her neglect had resulted in his loss.

"No, *piccola*. They must have been after the crown jewels."

"That's what Salvatore thought."

She looked at the opposite wall without seeing it, lost in thought. "You'll have to take the rest of the jewelry home with you. I don't think that's safe." She turned to Salvatore. He was the security expert and had insisted on forcing himself into her life. He could make himself useful now. "What shall we do?"

"Let me speak."

She stepped back, satisfied as the two men made arrangements for one of Salvatore's operatives to come and take possession of the jewelry.

She spoke briefly again with her boss before he left

the store, promising to be back when the vault's timed lock opened in the morning.

Returning to the storage cupboard, she perused the contents with more interest than the first time around. Now that she knew the inventory was safe and Signor di Adamo was not worried about her and Salvatore, she could consider dinner with more equanimity. Besides, she was hungry.

A round of cheese hung from a hook on the ceiling of the cupboard and she pulled it down. She also withdrew two bottles of mineral water with twist tops, a tin of tuna, crackers, and some small jars: olives, sundried tomatoes under oil and carrots under vinegar.

Stacking them together on the floor, she arranged the contents of the cupboard, so she could pull one of the shelves out to use as a table. Thankfully, Signor di Adamo had also included paper plates, utensils and napkins in his emergency store and she and Salvatore would not be reduced to serving with their fingers.

She arranged the crackers, tuna and cheese on two plates and put the small jars between them so both she and Salvatore could reach what they wanted. He hadn't said anything as she prepared the food, but he popped the tops off both bottles of mineral water and opened the other jars with quick precision.

He sat down on one side of the makeshift table while she gingerly settled on the floor on the other. "This is a far cry from what I intended our dinner to be tonight, *cara*."

Remembering his dinner reservation, she couldn't decide if reliving memories would have been worse or better than their enforced intimacy. "We haven't got much choice."

Salvatore shrugged, making the exposed muscles of his chest ripple in a very distracting way. OK, so it was warm, but buttoning up his shirt would not kill him.

"What do you know about my father's heart condition?" she asked as she sliced a thin sliver of cheese and put it on a cracker with one of the olives cut in half.

Salvatore sighed, as if his mind had been elsewhere. "It is not serious if he follows the doctor's recommendations and avoids stress."

Like that caused by worrying about his daughter's safety. She got the message without Salvatore having to spell it out.

"What happened?"

"He had a small episode a couple of months ago and ended up taking an emergency visit to the hospital. The doctor said that while the episode itself was not that serious, it was a harbinger of things to come if he did not change his lifestyle."

"And did he?"

Again the shrug and she wanted to just yell at him to button up his darn shirt. "Francesco has been working less, increasing his exercise, eating healthier."

"I'm sure Therese is making sure of that." Her stepmother loved her father very much.

"Sì."

"I still don't understand why he didn't tell me."

"I do not know."

If she hadn't been running from Salvatore for the

past year, she would have visited Sicily at least once and no doubt found out about her father's health then. Guilt weighed on her as she finished her small dinner. Cleaning up was easy and thankfully, with the help of the running water in the small bathroom's sink, they were able to avoid a lingering odor of tuna in the enclosed space.

Afterward, they settled back on the floor, but its ungiving hardness quickly grew uncomfortable. She shifted her sitting position, drawing her knees up to her chin, having long since abandoned her shoes.

"It is going to be very uncomfortable sleeping."

Her head came up at the sound of Salvatore's voice and her conscience pricked her.

She should tell him about the blow-up air mattress in the cupboard. The thing was, it was a single and they would have to share. It was the only option that made sense, but her mind rebelled at the prospect of sleeping in such close proximity to him. Even the thought of slumber on the hard floor had more appeal. It would definitely be better for her sanity.

Besides, there was no saying if it would still hold air after all the time it had sat unused on that shelf, she tried telling herself. In the end, her conscience would not let her keep it to herself however.

Grimacing, she stood up. "There's an air mattress."

His brow rose in question.

"You know, a blow-up thing we can use to sit on now."

"And sleep on later."

He caught on quick, but then he was a smart guy—about everything but her. "Yes."

''We will have to sleep together.''

There was nothing for it. She forced herself to nod. ''Yes.''

She almost offered to sleep on the floor at the look of satisfaction that crossed his features. ''Don't get any ideas, Salvatore. If you try anything, I'll push you right off the mattress, got it?''

CHAPTER SIX

IT WAS a ludicrous threat considering how much bigger he was than her, not to mention more dangerous, but he didn't laugh.

He did smile though. "You have made yourself clear."

She pulled out the mattress. There was no pump, so they took turns blowing into it to inflate it. Salvatore smiled the first time he took it from her, putting his lips where hers had been with deliberate movements, and she could almost feel his lips against hers. It was worse when she took it back from him because the intimacy of using the air spigot after Salvatore made her insides clench. She hid her reaction, but she felt as if he knew anyway.

Once they had it blown up, he pulled the blanket out and spread it over the mattress before they sat down on it.

It didn't give and there was no telltale hiss of escaping air. "I think it's going to hold." She wasn't sure if she was glad or disappointed by that fact. "I wish we had a pack of cards, or something."

"Are you bored with my company already, *dolcezza?*"

"No, of course not. It's just that..." She let her voice trail off.

He wasn't that dense. He knew what the problem was.

"I can think of something that would pass the time."

She stiffened and glared at him. "No way."

"What could be wrong with a game of Animal, Vegetable or Mineral?"

He'd been having her on, but she still couldn't see him playing such a simple game and said so.

"You forget the years I spent schooling in a very spartan environment."

And she acknowledged there were depths to this alpha male she knew nothing about.

So they played, but she was tired, having slept little the night before.

After her third yawn, he said, "I think you should sleep, *cara.*"

She didn't want to lie down, but it would have to happen some time. "Are you going to sleep?"

"It is that, pace, or sit on the hard floor. None of those appeal. I will sleep. I did not rest much last night."

"I'm sorry." Her nightmare had wakened him.

"Do not be. I have not slept well for the past year."

He took Sicilian guilt to Olympic levels, which did nothing for her own peace of mind. Sighing with a sense of inevitability, she went into the small bathroom and got ready for bed.

She came out and once again he was waiting. This time he was standing in just his trousers, his shirt dangling from one finger. "Put this on to sleep in. It will be more comfortable than your dress."

No doubt he was right, but still she balked. "I'll be fine."

"Do not be stubborn."

"My dress isn't that bad." It was longer and tighter than any of her nightgowns, but she could deal with it.

"You hate sleeping with anything wrapped around your legs."

The reminder of their former intimacy did nothing to improve her mood. "I'll survive this time."

He put the shirt around her shoulders. "There is no need." He stepped around her and entered the bathroom. "Elisa…"

"Yes?"

"I can think of nothing I would enjoy more than helping you change, *cara.*"

"Has anyone ever told you that you're too bossy?"

His answer was the quiet sliding shut of the bi-fold door. She didn't know if he would follow through on his threat to help her change, but on the likely chance he would, she made quick work of slipping out of her dress and bra and putting his shirt on. She buttoned the buttons all the way up, but the collar was big enough that it still showed the dips and hollows of her collarbone.

Afterward, she went to the mattress to lie down. He had laid his coat down on one side and she knew it was there for a buffer between her skin and the velour-covered plastic of the mattress. She considered sleeping on the opposite side out of defiance, but decided against it. He'd put her beside the wall so she wouldn't fall off the mattress either and somehow his concern touched instead of irritated her.

She snuggled down onto his coat, pretending to herself that the scent of him was not having an impact on her emotions or physical comfort. Waiting for him to come out of the bathroom, she pulled the light blanket over herself, more to cover her bare legs than because she was cold.

He came out a few minutes later. "Do you want me to leave the light on?"

It was a small enclosure. They both knew it well enough to find the bathroom if they needed it and they would sleep better in the dark. "No."

He pressed a button and the dull glow of the emergency light went out.

She waited for him to join her on the bed, tense with an emotion between dread and anticipation. When he did, he put his arm around her waist and the other under her head like a pillow, cuddling up to her back as if they were still lovers.

She stiffened with rejection and tried to push out of his arms. "Salvatore!"

He tightened his hold. "Be reasonable, *cara,* the mattress is small. It is the only comfortable position for sleeping."

"But—"

"I promised I would not accost you. Can you not trust me this much?"

Why the question should stir her emotions, she did not know. She started to say something again.

"Shh…" Soft lips kissed her temple. "Sleep. That is all." Then, nothing.

He made no attempt to take advantage of their position and eventually she relaxed, feeling more secure than she had in months. Incredibly, she slept.

When she woke, the darkness was absolute.

Slowly, memory of where she was penetrated her mind, but something was missing.

The warmth of Salvatore's body surrounding hers. The blanket was tucked around her, as if pressed carefully there by someone else. But no Salvatore.

She listened, but could hear no sound from the lavatory. Besides, in the absolute darkness, light would filter through the cracks of the bi-fold door if he was in there. She could hear his breathing, but not where it was coming from.

She sat up, groggy from sleep, the blanket falling to her waist. "Salvatore?"

"*Sì, cara?*"

Her voice had been husky from slumber, but his was crisp, as if he'd been awake a while.

"Why aren't you sleeping?"

His laugh was harsh. "You have reason to doubt it, but I have some honor."

"Did I say I doubted it?"

"It is not necessary. I know what you think of me."

She rubbed at her eyes, but of course that made no improvement on the impenetrable darkness. "Your honor isn't letting you sleep?" Nothing was making sense to her still sleep-fuddled mind.

"I want you."

"I know." He'd made that patently clear and even half asleep, she could hear the sensual edge to his tone.

"I cannot lie next to your delectable body for one minute longer and not take you."

The admission cost him. She could hear it in his

voice. He hated being subject to such strong physical need. His next words confirmed it.

"I swore after Sofia that no woman would hold me in sexual thrall like that again."

"You don't like being out of control." He might not believe it, but she found no satisfaction in enthralling him sexually. Straight sexual hunger was nothing compared to love and respect.

"I grew up learning self-discipline and control in the face of circumstances that would be impossible for many people."

"And the idea of a mere woman breaking through that terrifies you, doesn't it?"

"I am not afraid." She couldn't see him, but she could sure hear his affront.

"Bad choice of words."

"I am not over there seducing you. I do have some self-control where you are concerned."

But not a lot and he'd had to get out of the bed to exercise it. She didn't rub that in, however. She had realized some time yesterday that she got no pleasure out of hurting him.

"I'm sorry."

"Sorry enough to let me make love to you?"

She laughed at the absurdity of the question. "No way would you ever be able to accept sex based on pity."

"You would be surprised."

His desire beat at her like a pulsing base in an orchestra of sensual composition.

Her own body's needs warred with the thoughts going through her mind. This man had abandoned her and their baby. She could not trust him with her body again.

But he had also come back.

That fact had not struck her until a few months ago. *He had been there when she was losing the baby because he had come to her apartment to see her.* She didn't know why and for a long time had not cared, but now she wondered.

"Why did you come back?"

"You said you were pregnant with my child."

"You didn't believe it was yours."

"I realized it did not matter."

"What do you mean?"

"You believed the baby was mine. I would have married you. The baby would have been mine."

"You were prepared to marry me even though you thought I might be pregnant with another man's child?"

"This is the truth."

Unbelievable! "You weren't willing to do that for Sofia."

"I was younger. Hot-headed. And she lied to me."

"You thought I lied to you." He'd said so.

"You told me what you wanted to be true. It is not the same. You believed it."

While what he was saying touched her, the fact he still doubted her hurt. "It was *your* baby."

He didn't reply for a long time, and when the words did come they weren't the ones she wanted to hear. "I let you down."

"Yes."

"I am sorry."

"It doesn't help."

"I know."

But was that entirely true?

After learning about Sofia Pennini, Elisa appreciated better why Salvatore had not trusted her. An experience like that would make any man wary when his lover told him she was pregnant with his child. Her father's assertion Elisa was just like her mother had justifiably fueled Salvatore's distrust.

So, yes, she understood why he believed what he did, but it made little difference to her emotion-deprived heart. The simple truth remained. If he had loved her, he would have *wanted* the baby to be his, not been afraid it was so. He would have believed her. He never would have left.

For a brief time, in her naiveté, she had believed he loved her. He'd wined and dined her. Flattered her. And he'd bedded her. In the end it had been that easy. Over her vacation in Sicily, she had fallen helplessly in love with Salvatore. She'd had no hope of resisting his blatant seduction when he looked her up in Milan.

Stupidly, she had mistaken his passion for love. She had ended up pregnant with his child and had only then come to appreciate her mistake. He had not believed her that the baby was his and she'd miscarried. Now they had this *thing* between them that was both too big to dismiss and yet nothing at all.

"How long have you been sitting there?"

"I do not know."

"I can move to the floor if you like. I've got your coat to lie on anyway."

"No."

"It's bound to be more comfortable for me than it is for you."

"No."

"You're so stubborn and you're too macho for your own good."

"You think I am macho?" There was humor in his voice, which was a real improvement over the almost desperate tone he'd had earlier, or the dead tone he'd used when he apologized.

"*Please,* Salvatore. You're so macho, you could bottle and sell it. Not only are you a good head taller than most Sicilian men, but you also have more muscles than any tycoon has a right to." And the way he'd been flashing them earlier was still affecting her breathing when she thought about it. "You're trained to fight like a commando and you practically define the word virile. It's enough to make a woman swoon."

The only warning she had that he had moved was the faint sound of fabric brushing against fabric and then he was there. Next to her on the mattress, his face so close to hers that his breath brushed her skin.

"I define the word virile?"

Perhaps that had been a dumb thing to admit, but it was no use lying now. "Yes."

"But you will not let me share your bed."

"I didn't kick you out of the bed. You left because you were afraid of seducing me."

"You admit I could seduce you?"

"I'm not admitting anything. It's your own worries that had you sitting on the hard floor in the middle of the night."

"Fear. Worry. You make me sound like an old woman."

Nervous laughter huffed out of her. "I don't think so."

His lips brushed her cheek. "Maybe you want to be seduced," he whispered, the words a caress against her skin.

Warmth pooled in her inner places while she cursed the darkness that seemed to magnify the electricity of his touch. "N-no."

"Once again and with meaning." His lips played with hers and she couldn't seem to work up enough self-preservation to tell him to stop. "You want me, *cara*. Admit it."

Her only defense lay in the truth. "Of course I want you. What red-blooded woman wouldn't? What do you think I've been saying? But my body doesn't always want what is best for my mind or my heart."

His warm, masculine hand curled around her waist. "This time it does. Trust me, Elisa. I will not hurt you again."

How could he help it? He didn't love her and that in itself hurt. It shouldn't. She didn't love him anymore. How could she after all he had done? She should be able to take her pleasure the way he did, with no emotional entanglement. Only she knew she couldn't, probably not with any man, but most definitely not with him. What she didn't know was why.

Breathing in the scent of her body's only acknowledged mate, realization blinded her like a lightning bolt in the darkness of the vault. *She still loved him.* Despite the way he had rejected her, she would always love him.

No. Her breathing turned shallow from fear. She'd thought her emotions were dead. Safely buried under a wall of pain so she couldn't hurt any more. *She didn't want to love him.*

His mouth pressed against the corner of her lips, his tongue flicking out to taste her and then retreating. "Please, *dolcezza,* let me pleasure you."

The shock of her inner revelation combined with the physical sensations overwhelming her in the absolute darkness of the vault. And her mind stopped functioning, short-circuited by the words and tone that promised so much.

Her head turned and her lips sought his blindly, needing more than that brief touch.

CHAPTER SEVEN

LIPS hard with passion closed over hers.

Want, need and love coalesced inside her, creating an overwhelming ache that was both physical and emotional. A sense of emptiness in the core of her femininity craved the filling of his flesh. Her heart fed on the need in his voice, the tension in his touch that attested his need for her.

A year ago she had exulted in this hunger that was so much more than mere physical lust, but now it terrified her. She knew what pain lay beyond the satiation of her senses.

But even her fear of the depth of emotion elicited by his kiss could not stifle the need, nor her body and heart's demand it be met.

While her mouth feasted on the taste of her lover so long denied her, her body shifted against him in voluptuous abandon. He groaned, his hands closing convulsively on her. She pressed against his naked chest, digging her fingers into the short curling hair and muscled contours.

Her eyes were open, but she couldn't see anything. All she could do was feel.

His fingers undoing the buttons on the shirt she wore. His mouth staking a claim on hers. His heart beating an erratic rhythm against her hand. The pebble-hard bump of his male nipple. Then the feel of his hands cupping her naked breasts, kneading them with sensual urgency.

She let her hand slide down to measure his already hard male flesh through his trousers.

Moaning like a man in torture, he broke the kiss and she sensed his head falling back in abandonment to the pleasure of her touch. His hands continued caressing her breasts in what felt like a mindless pattern of squeeze and release...squeeze and release.

He strained against the fly of his trousers, letting her know without words that his need was as much as or greater than her own. Carefully, with one hand, she undid his fastening and pulled the zip down slowly enough to make him groan again.

"*Sì.* Touch me, *cara.* I need your hand on me."

But she didn't touch him.

She peeled the fabric away, cautious not to so much as brush his rigid flesh with the backs of her fingers. Then she pushed the trousers down his hips, waiting for him to move so she could slide them all the way off. Taking her time, she was careful not to let even the tip of his shaft into contact with any part of her body.

She loved teasing him like this.

"You are driving me mad."

"Do you mind?" she asked with gentle mockery. "Maybe you want me to stop."

"No!"

She smiled and, using the same maddening caution, she removed his silk boxer shorts.

She could feel his big body shudder and her own was shaking. Her nipples were so hard, the skin felt stretched unbearably taut and her breasts swelled in his hands.

"Salvatore..." She sighed out his name, glad for the darkness that hid the emotions swirling through her from his penetrating gaze.

"You want me." He made it a statement and she did not bother to answer.

Her body was doing a fine job all on its own. She was drenched with desire between her legs, the flesh there engorged and throbbing.

She touched his face like a blind woman, trying to see with her hands. He let her, his body curiously still, as she allowed her fingertips to roam over him from the angles of his handsome face to biceps bulging with sexual tension, to the even ridges of muscle on his abdomen.

He sucked in air as she traced the line of his pelvis and once again she smiled. In this way, he was not so in control.

She stopped with her fingertip pressing into him just above his throbbing erection. She could feel the heat radiating off of him even though she could not see the familiar evidence of masculine arousal.

"I wonder what it is you want?"

"You." His voice was guttural. "Just you, you teasing little witch."

For right now she took the words at face value, pretending they meant what her heart longed for them to mean, but she didn't move.

They stayed that way for several seconds, both of them anticipating the touch that was next to come.

When she could withstand the self-inflicted torment no longer, she curled her fingers around him with possessive pleasure and reveled in the primitive sound that tore out of his throat. Strong hands convulsively gripped her breasts. The pressure increased her own excitement and made her nipples ache for the kind of caresses they had come to expect from this incredibly sexy man.

She pleasured him as he had once taught her to do, unaware that his expressive passion had guided innocent hands to the touch that gave him the most gratification.

Without any warning, even the preliminary touching she'd always taken for granted, a hot, insistent mouth closed over one of her stiff peaks. She cried out from the shock of it.

He started sucking. Hard. She arched toward him, the apex of her thighs brushing against his solid, broad tip. The thin silk barrier of her panties might not even have been there.

The touch was so electric, so wanted, so *much* after a year-long desert of stimulation she shuddered and cried out in a mini-culmination.

He reared back, his breath rasping from his throat. "You are perfect for me. No woman has ever been so perfect."

She only vaguely registered the compliment, her entire attention centered on the pleasure still rippling through her body.

Then he was pushing the shirt off her shoulders, guiding her backward so he could dispense with her panties. Expecting him to come down on top of her, she was confused when instead she felt the change in the pressure in the air mattress as he got off of it.

"Where are you going?"

"I want to see you." She heard a click and then the soft glow of the emergency lighting filled the vault.

After the absolute black, her eyes closed against what felt like a harsh glare and it took several seconds before she could open them and keep them open. By then he was back on the mattress and looking at her.

His dark eyes were pools of black fire burning in his face as he soaked in the vision of her lying there, open to him.

"*Bellisima*. You are the most beautiful woman I have ever seen. An angel of perfection."

His lavish praise was something that had shocked her at first when this Sicilian tycoon had become her lover, but now she adored it.

Warmed by his blatant approval, she let her eyes feast on his nudity too.

The subdued lighting made his bronzed skin even darker, but did nothing to hide the gorgeous sculpting of his features and build. He was everything that defined virile, just as she'd said. So much a man, such an amazing lover.

She looked at him through her lashes, her lips slightly parted in a pout. "Are you going to come get me?"

He didn't laugh as she expected, as he had many times when she had taunted him like that. Instead his face contorted as if with pain and he came to her in a rush. A low growl vibrated in his throat in response to her feminine challenge.

All thought of playing fled as his body invaded hers in one smooth stroke that left them both panting.

He didn't move, but held himself rigid above her for so long, she asked, "Is something wrong?"

"No." He kissed her, hard and thoroughly. "Something is right. Very right."

It felt that way to her too and she wrapped her arms and legs around him, letting him set a pace that would bring them both the fulfillment they craved.

He didn't go hard and fast as she expected, but started an agonizingly slow rocking, pulling almost completely out before pressing forward again, sheathing himself in her slow centimeter by centimeter. A few minutes of the sensual torment and she was crying out for more, but he refused.

"No, *dolcezza*. It must last. This first time must go on forever."

She wasn't going to survive five more minutes, much less forever. She unhooked her legs and dug her heels into the mattress, bowing her body upward and forcing him to sink into her to the hilt. She gyrated wildly with her hips, needing the friction between their bodies to complete the starburst of pleasure just out of her reach.

When it came, it was like a supernova going off in her head and body. She screamed so loud, her throat felt raw, but his shout of completion was even louder.

Her ears rang, her body trembled, her muscles ached from contractions so intense they had made the now lit vault go black around her. She collapsed back on the mattress and he came with her, covering her body completely with his own.

He said something she didn't understand.

She was so tired. "Sleep..." she said, her voice slurred.
If he answered, she did not hear.

Elisa woke, sure she was still asleep and dreaming,
for only that scenario could explain how her naked
body could be wrapped tightly against the equally
nude body of her former lover. Even in the darkness,
she knew his scent, his form, the very feel of him.
She would never forget it.

"Buono mattina, cara," a husky voice rumbled
against her right temple.

She went completely rigid as the events of the night
before came back to her. She had let him make love
to her. No, not just let him. She had begged him in
the end.

"How do you know it's morning?" He must have
turned off the light again after she fell asleep because
the darkness in the vault was absolute.

"My watch has a night reading function."

"Oh." Stupid, inane conversation for the morning
after, but then she didn't know what meaningful thing
she could say. "What time is it?"

"Eight-fifteen. We slept late."

What they'd done had little to do with sleeping.
Then she realized Signor di Adamo would be there
when the vault door opened...in less than an hour. If
the door opened right now, there would be no hiding
what she and Salvatore had been doing. She sat
straight up, panic clawing through her.

"We have to get dressed."

His hand brushed her bare stomach, making already
tight muscles clench further. "Relax. We have plenty
of time."

The scent of their lovemaking permeated the air around them. "How can you tell me to relax? Do you think I want my boss to know I spent the night with his security consultant?"

"I am your lover. Why not?"

She could tell him why not, the arrogant— Her thoughts stopped mid-tirade as she became more aware of the sticky wetness between her legs. She knew this feeling. She'd had it once before. The first time they'd made love. It had a distinctly different quality from the times after when they made love using a condom.

"You didn't use anything," she screeched at him, scrambling to her feet.

Trying to get off the mattress so she could get to the light switch, she tripped and started to fall. She yelped, but didn't make contact with the hard floor because two strong hands pulled her back onto the bed, right into his lap.

"Stop this. You will hurt yourself."

"You didn't use a condom!" she condemned him again.

"No, I did not." He didn't even sound remotely sorry.

"Why not?"

"One reason is I did not have one with me. I was not prepared to be locked in a vault all night with you, *dolcezza.*"

Sweet? She'd give him sweet! "One reason? What was the other? You were so out of control with lust you didn't think of it?" Right. More likely he just hadn't cared. After all, he wasn't the one who had ended up pregnant the last time. "You didn't even try to pull out at the crucial moment."

How could she have been so stupid?

"I did not think of such a thing." And his tone of voice implied he wouldn't have been impressed with the thought if he'd had it. "I *was* out of control. So were you, no?"

"That's no excuse!" she said instead of answering the provocative question.

"I was not attempting to excuse it."

No, he hadn't been. Not that that made any sense. OK, so he wasn't the one who'd got pregnant the first time they had unprotected sex, but he was a responsible man. She knew it even when she wanted to pretend otherwise. So, why wasn't he upset?

She would have expected some sort of remorse prompted by his over-active guilt gene.

She tipped her head back, trying to see what he was thinking, but the pitch black gave her no clue. "We can't have this conversation in the dark."

"I do not suggest we have this conversation now at all." He moved his arm and a brief glow illuminated his wrist. It was almost eerie in the otherwise complete blackness. "You have barely a half an hour to wash and prepare yourself to meet your employer."

Oh, no, he was right! Their conversation, her anger and confusion, they would all have to wait. She couldn't bear the idea of being caught naked in bed with Salvatore by her boss. She tried getting up again, but he set her firmly to one side.

"I will get the light. Then you may move without doing yourself an injury."

"Too bad you didn't show such refined protective instincts last night." She was doing quick mental calculations, and just as the light came on she realized something terrifying.

"It's the middle of my cycle." She stared up at him, immobilized by the utter certainty they had made another baby the night before. "Last time I got pregnant when it wasn't even the right time. What chance have I now that it won't happen?"

His face clenched. "Do not take on as if the world has ended. It has not."

Not his world maybe, but then his world hadn't altered last time either. Only hers had. She'd had her heart ripped right out of her chest by his rejection and then all over again by the loss of their baby.

She didn't say anything, just looked up at him, feeling the tragedy of her life pressing in around her in stifling waves.

He said something harsh under his breath and bent down on his haunches beside her. "It will be all right, *cara*. Trust me on this."

She stared at him, not seeing him, but rather an image of herself once again pregnant. Once again alone. She shook her head. "I can't trust you."

"You can." He tugged her to her feet and then kissed her hard on her mouth. Letting her go, he said, "Go wash yourself and dress. I will clean up out here."

Get dressed. Yes, she had to dress before the timed lock on the vault released and let the rest of the world in again to see what an idiot she'd been.

Salvatore swore as he watched Elisa walk toward the bathroom, her body bowed like that of an old woman. She was terrified of once more becoming pregnant

with his child. He had seen it in her eyes, but he had
not expected it. He had told her he now knew he had
made a mistake in his reaction to the news a year ago.
Did she not realize he would never abandon her
again?

She belonged to him and he would take care of her.

Starting now. It took him only seconds to dress.
His shirt smelled of her and his body reacted in a
predictable fashion to the feminine fragrance teasing
his nostrils. Ignoring his desire, he folded up his suit
coat, hiding the evidence of their lovemaking. He de-
flated the mattress as well, putting it and the blanket
back in the storage cupboard.

A snicking sound indicated the vault was unlocking
as Elisa emerged from the bathroom. Her skin was
too pale and her pupils too dilated for his liking, but
he could not reassure her the way she needed to be
reassured in front of Signor di Adamo.

She avoided making eye contact as she slipped her
shoes on and then stood, waiting for the door to finish
unlocking. He let her get away with it. For now.

Just as he had promised the evening before, Signor
di Adamo was waiting on the other side once the door
was open, his expression filled with deep concern.

He pulled Elisa into an exuberant hug. "*Piccola.*
You are all right. Praise the good God above." He
held her away from him, no doubt noting what
Salvatore had earlier, but giving it an entirely different interpretation. He shook his gray head. "This has
been too much."

He looked at Salvatore. "Arrangements must be
made."

Salvatore nodded. "*Sì*. We will talk, but first I must make some calls."

The old man agreed and led Elisa back into his apartment.

While Signor di Adamo fussed over her, Salvatore called his office and ordered two more operatives and then made arrangements for himself and Elisa to travel to Sicily later that afternoon.

When he informed Elisa she was to return to the hotel with his operatives while he and her boss discussed what was to be done about security for the store, she did not even put up a token protest.

Which, more than anything else could have, revealed her continued state of shock from realizing they had made love without using protection. He grimaced as he watched her go from the store. She had only more shocks to come.

Elisa stepped out of the shower and started toweling off.

She was in her own tiny bathroom in her small but cheerful apartment.

Once they had left the jewelry store, she had informed the operatives for Vitale Security that she wanted to go home. They had balked, but she'd remained adamant, simply refusing to get out of the car until the driver took her to her apartment. Salvatore would have picked her up and carried her, she had no doubt, but she was equally sure he would fire another man for doing so.

His operatives had apparently understood this as well and eventually took her where she wanted to go. Home.

She needed the familiar.

Upon arrival at her apartment she had tried to dismiss them, but it had been their turn to be obstinate. So she'd left them in the hall and still felt guilty about it, but not enough to invite them inside her small home.

After taking them something to drink and offering them chairs from her dinette set, which they refused, she had left them to do their sentinel duty and gone to take a shower. She'd needed to be clean and she could not stand the thought of strangers in her tiny apartment while she did something so intimate.

She wasn't in the mood for company period. Her mind was functioning again, but barely. The thought of putting on a calm façade for the two men was anathema to her, so she left them in the hall and didn't even care if her neighbors thought it odd she had two armed guards outside her door.

She dressed and brushed her long hair into a wet ponytail. Then she made herself some coffee, all the while her mind spinning with the reality of the night before.

She had let Salvatore make love to her.

Unprotected sex.

The words pulsed in her brain like a blinking neon sign. Garish. Loud. Impossible to ignore.

She'd gotten good and mad at Salvatore, but she was the idiot who had allowed him admission to her body—a man who had proven his only feelings for her were lust. She hadn't once considered the possibility of pregnancy. Had not thought to ask about protection. Which was gross negligence on her part, or just plain insanity. She didn't know which.

She went to take a sip of her coffee, but put the cup down again, remembering something she'd read during her pregnancy a year ago. She got up from her small dinette table and dumped her coffee down the drain.

Some doctors thought caffeine wasn't good for babies, and if she was pregnant she wasn't going to lose this baby.

She wasn't.

She pressed her hand into her lower abdomen. Did she harbor Salvatore's baby in her womb? Was she nurturing new life?

She was still confused, still devastated by the very possibility of conception. Nevertheless a fog that had shrouded her mind and heart since the involuntary termination of her first pregnancy began to dissipate. A very tiny spark of warmth began to glow deep in her heart.

The fear was still there. So was the anger. The pain had not miraculously disappeared, but underneath it all a sense of life and living she had thought gone forever furled into fragile being.

"You look lost in thought, *cara mia.*"

She spun away from the sink to find Salvatore less than ten feet away. Her gaze skittered to the door.

"I sent them away."

"How did you get in?"

His dark eyes looked wary. "You did not answer my knock."

She hadn't heard him come in either. She had been *very* lost in thought. "So?"

"So, I picked the lock. The door is not very secure. I am not happy about this. You could be accosted in your sleep and never even hear the perpetrator trying to get in.''

She shook her head.

"I assure you it is true.''

"I wasn't denying it.'' Why had she never realized that the man liked to argue? Probably because before, the arguments, even small disagreements like this, had ended in bed. A place she had thoroughly enjoyed being with him. Before. "I was trying to clear my mind.''

His mouth quirked. "Did it work?''

"No.'' She wasn't sure what would. It was as if her life was just out of focus, but for the first time in months…she wondered if it was going to stay that way. "Why didn't you just knock again? *Louder.*''

"I was worried.''

She saw that, in the faintly gray cast to his freshly shaven face, in the tiny lines at the corners of his eyes.

"Did you think I was going to do something stupid?''

"I did not think you would harm yourself, but I did think you might disappear again.''

"You looked for me the last time.'' She'd wondered if he had.

"*Sì.* But you could not be found.''

No need to wonder how he felt about that. Chagrin and residual anger were clear in his expression and tone.

"So, you picked my lock to make sure I was still in here. What was I supposed to do—climb out through the window?'' She wasn't anywhere near as big as Salvatore, but even so, such a thing would have been a real feat.

"You are resourceful."

"I see." Curiously touched by his estimation of her intelligence and abilities, she turned her head to hide her expression from him. "Would you like some coffee?"

"I had coffee at the hotel. I want to talk."

Yes, she could tell he'd gone back to the hotel, for not only had he shaved, but his damp hair indicated he had also showered and his suit was fresh. He was wearing a tie today.

Why that detail stuck in her mind she did not know.

Maybe because it was easier to focus on the mundane than the possibility—no, *probability*—she was pregnant again.

"What do you want to talk about?"

"The likelihood we will be parents in nine months' time."

CHAPTER EIGHT

THAT had her looking at him.

He wasn't smiling. No teasing. He'd meant it, but then possible parenthood was no joking matter.

"I suppose this time you'll believe the baby is yours, or are you wondering if I've had a lover in the past year?"

"I know you have not."

"How? Have you been having one of your operatives spying on me?"

Dull color burnished his cheekbones and her eyes widened. "You have!"

"You would not see me. I had to know you were all right. So, I had you checked up on."

"Well, unless you had me followed twenty-four-seven, you can't know if I've been faithful to you, can you?"

Why had she put it like that? There was nothing to be faithful to. They weren't married. They weren't even dating any longer.

"I just know," he said, ignoring her slip of the tongue.

"What, now security tycoons are psychic too?"

It was a juvenile jab and his expression said he thought so too. "This arguing is getting us nowhere."

"Maybe we have nowhere to go."

"On the contrary. We leave for Sicily in an hour."

"What are you talking about? We aren't going to

Sicily.'' She put her hands on her hips and gave him her best glower. ''I have a job. Signor di Adamo is counting on me.''

''Adamo Jewelers will be closed until the auction.''

Her heart contracted with pain at what that would mean. ''No. That will ruin his business. He'll lose everything.''

''This will not happen.''

''Says you?'' she challenged him.

''*Sì*. I say. I have worked things out with your boss. My company will finish installing the new security system while the store is closed as well as seeing to some necessary structural and wiring changes in his building.''

''He can't afford that.'' She should know. She did the books and Signor di Adamo was hanging on by a financial thread.

''I have taken care of it.''

If Salvatore had worked around her boss's pride to the extent that Signor di Adamo allowed him to do these things, then he had been ten times more politic with him than he'd ever been with her.

''What about the crown jewels?''

''They will be transported to an undisclosed location for storage until the auction.''

''I suppose your company is supplying security for the auction now as well.'' Not that she really minded. She hadn't known how she was going to handle security for the prestigious guest list, much less the jewels. It was just his high-handed way of handling things that got to her.

''*Sì*.''

''I don't understand why I have to go to Sicily,

then. I'm not at risk if the jewels aren't in my keeping."

"And how are would-be thieves to know that you and Signor di Adamo no longer have access to the jewels?"

They couldn't exactly put out an ad in the paper. She bit her lip and stared out the window, then looked back at Salvatore. "I guess I just assumed that if they knew we had them, they'd know when we didn't."

"The world is not such a simple place, *amore*."

Something snapped inside her at the use of that endearment. "You know, I've put up with you calling me sweet and darling. I don't like it—" and her heart called her a liar "—but I tolerate it. They're just words to an Italian man. I know that, but don't you ever call me love. Got it? Love has nothing to do with our relationship."

She wasn't going to fool herself into believing love prompted his protectiveness or concern for her. Sicilian guilt and obligation to a family friend mixed with a lot of red-hot desire were the extent of his feelings toward her and she'd do well to remember that.

His expression could have been set in cement. "You are saying you no longer love me. I know this."

"And you don't love me, so let's not play games."

"I was not aware I was playing any game."

"Then stop using endearments, would you?"

"You are dear to me."

"I'm your guilty burden, you mean."

Another layer of cement poured over his expression. "Did last night feel like guilt?"

She couldn't deal with what it had felt like. She had to deal with reality. "Last night was about two people overcome by lust to the extent that they both forgot birth control."

"I did not forget."

"Right." She glared at him. Men, especially macho men like Salvatore, had a hard time admitting when they'd messed up. "You just decided to forgo any attempt at preventing the conception of a child."

"This is so."

"What?" She could not have heard what she thought she had just heard. No way. Not possible.

"I chose to do nothing to prevent pregnancy."

"You said you didn't have a condom with you." Was that whisper-soft voice sounding so stunned hers?

"I did not, but I could have made love differently to you."

"But you didn't."

"I did not."

She plopped down into the dining chair she had vacated earlier, her legs going wobbly on her. "Because you thought real men didn't pull out, or something?"

His eyes mocked her words. "That thought was not in my mind."

"What thought was in your mind, then? You can't tell me you wanted me to get pregnant."

"But I did. I do."

She could actually feel the blood draining from her face as shock made her heart skip a beat and her breathing shallow. "You want me to get pregnant?"

she asked again, incapable of voicing any other concept.

"*Sì.*"

"*But why?*"

"There are many reasons."

"Name one."

"Your health."

"You think I'll be healthier pregnant? But that's absurd."

"Not so. I spoke to a doctor after your miscarriage. He warned me you might have what is termed post-partum depression."

She'd heard of after-the-baby blues, but she hadn't had a baby and said so.

"The hormones that become imbalanced can do so after a miscarriage as well. It was clear you were still sad, still not functioning under your normal faculties. Not only have you stayed away from other men this year, but you have also stopped socializing altogether. You moved from your apartment, but you never go back to visit the friends you had in your old building. You refuse every invitation from Signor di Adamo to share a meal with his family."

"I suppose your spies told you that too," she cried, stung by his assessment of her.

"No. Your boss. He is worried also, but he thinks the sadness is due to our breakup."

"It was! And to losing the baby. I don't have some sort of chemical imbalance you need to fix by getting me pregnant."

"Perhaps, but the grief counselor I spoke to also said that having another baby would help you with the grief over losing our first one."

"You talked to a grief counselor *and* a doctor about me?"

"I wanted to know why you were so adamant in your refusal to see or speak to me."

"Because you hurt me and I didn't want you in my life any more. I could have told you that!"

A muscle in his jaw ticked, but he didn't get angry. "There was more to it than that."

"So, you thought you'd fix what your imagination told you was wrong with me by getting me pregnant?" No matter how many times she said it, it still sounded unbelievable.

"I also believed you would agree to marry me once you knew you again carried my child."

"So now the baby was yours?" she asked scathingly in an attempt to mask the other emotions swirling through her.

"You say it is so. I should not have doubted you."

But then he hadn't loved her and doubt found a fertile ground in the distrust he'd harbored toward women since Sofia.

"You can't force me into marrying you."

His shrug was anything but reassuring. It as good as said, *Yeah, right, whatever you say, but I am Salvatore di Vitale and I know how to get what I want.*

And right now…he wanted her to marry him.

Salvatore watched the emotions flow across her expressive features. None of them were even remotely related to joy at the prospect of marriage to him.

That made him angry. So, he had made a mistake.

It happened. That she should dismiss all that they shared because of it was ludicrous.

"We have a lot going for us."

"Your distrust of women, my distrust of you and lots of lust. That is not my idea of a recipe for a happy life together."

Her sarcasm was wearing away at his good intentions.

"Oh, yes, and let us not forget your guilt. The only real reason you want to marry me in the first place."

Why did she have to keep bringing up his guilt? Of course he felt guilty toward her. He had hurt her, his anger had caused the loss of their baby. He would never forget that fact. Did not know if he could ever forgive himself.

"I have forgotten nothing."

Like the fact that at one time she had wanted his love. Now she did not care. In a way, he was glad. He did not know if he had this love to give her. He'd thought he loved Sofia, but had realized later his pride had been lacerated, not his heart.

What he felt for Elisa was bound up with the overwhelming desire his body had to mate with hers. Was that love?

Probably not the kind of love a woman would understand or want. It wasn't flowery and romantic. What he felt around her was too elemental. In the final picture, love did not come into it. He owed her a baby. He owed her the security of marriage and a family.

"You will marry me."

"I'll do as I please." She looked both incredibly fragile and stubbornly defiant.

"May I suggest it please you to get ready for our trip to Sicily? If we do not leave on time, my pilot will lose his take-off slot at the airport."

She glared. "I don't have to go to Sicily with you."

"And those after the crown jewels?"

"I can go somewhere else, a place neither you nor the bad guys can find me."

Panic lanced through him that she might do just that. "Your father would worry if he did not know where you were."

"Then I'll tell him."

"And he will tell me."

Her small hands made tight fists against her thighs. "Not if I tell him not to." She didn't sound completely convinced of that fact.

And she should not be. "No father is going to allow his daughter to remain unprotected when there is any risk she could be hurt by her own stubborn independence."

"So, I won't tell him!"

"And risk causing him another heart episode in his worry for you?"

An hour later, buckled into a seat on Salvatore's private jet, Elisa stewed. *What a Class A manipulator.*

He'd known exactly what buttons to push to get her to agree to go to Sicily with him, but, even knowing she was being manipulated, she would not change her mind. Papa would worry. She knew that. He was sick and she could not stand it if she was the reason something truly bad happened with his health.

Besides, she wanted to know why he had told

Salvatore she was like Shawna. She was tired of just accepting the outsider's role in her family. She wanted something more and it began with her father's trust and belief that she was every bit as good a daughter as Annemarie. Somehow, she would get him to see that.

She knew deep down that he loved her.

She needed to feel that love now, not just be aware of its existence.

How different these thoughts were from the ones she'd always harbored about love and family. Shawna had raised her to depend only on herself, to rely on no one else physically or emotionally, because other people let you down. Elisa had learned the truth of that statement early on, right at Shawna's knee.

Here Salvatore was, invading her space, demanding she rely on him. He wanted her to depend on him, to trust him, but how could she? He'd shown her that, just as with the other people she loved in her life, she had only a minor role to play in his. That of lover, but not beloved.

He wanted to marry her because he felt guilty. If it had been for any other reason, she would have jumped at the chance to build a life with him, to have the family she had never had. She craved the closeness she saw in other families, the relationship that existed between her father, Therese and Annemarie.

She was livid with Salvatore for tempting her with what she wanted most in the world, but knew she could not really have.

Because in a marriage without love, she wouldn't belong to him any more than she had ever really belonged with Shawna or her father.

*   *   *

They were on the road that led to the di Vitale estate outside of Palermo before Elisa realized Salvatore was not taking her to her father's house.

Instead they pulled past the iron-gate entrance to his palatial home.

"Why have we come here first?"

Salvatore's profile was grim, as it had been since she had agreed with little grace to accompany him to Sicily. "You are staying with me."

"No, I am not."

He pulled the car to a stop in front of the huge old house. It looked like something straight out of a European guidebook, a classic example of the opulent Mediterranean villa, home of the wealthy from the previous century.

Salvatore got out of the car and came around to open her door. Although his big body shaded her from the sun, hot air blasted her as the climate-controlled coolness of the car poured out through the open door.

She made no move to get out, leaving her safety belt buckled. "I'm not going inside."

He sighed. "I got very little sleep last night, *cara*."

That had her frowning. "Whose fault is that?"

"Yours."

She gasped out her outrage at that. "I didn't seduce you last night."

"Did you not?" His gaze traveled over her like seeking hands. "Your very presence in the same space is a seduction to my senses. Surely you know this."

"It's not my fault you didn't get any sleep," she

maintained stubbornly, not sure how she felt about his admission.

"*It is.* Therefore, you must also accept the results. I am out of patience. I wish to refresh myself, to relax in my home. I will not stand beside this car arguing with you. Come into the house now, Elisa, or I will carry you there, but be assured you are coming."

His words elicited not the least amount of surprise, but they did make her angry. "You're being a bully."

"I am being practical. Are you coming?"

She didn't want to know how she would react to his touch should he carry out his threat so she undid her seat belt with a jerky movement. "You should have six younger siblings, the way you like to boss people around."

His bark of laughter was short. "My parents wanted more, but Mamma died before that goal was achieved."

"Your father never remarried."

"No."

She climbed out of the car. "He must have loved your mother very much."

"He says so."

She cast a glance at Salvatore. "You don't believe him?"

"I do not disbelieve him."

"But you can't comprehend that kind of love?" she guessed.

He shrugged. "Not really, no."

Which as good as told her in no uncertain terms that what he felt for her was nothing like the emotion his father had had for his mother. "I wish I couldn't," she muttered to herself as she followed him inside.

He stopped in the cavernous hall and looked back at her. "What did you say?"

"Nothing." As if she was admitting it to him. That was not happening. She looked around in silence.

She loved the warm, old-world feel of the di Vitale home Salvatore shared with his father and grandfather. No grandmother, Elisa mused, the woman had died before he was even born. It struck her that Salvatore had had very little feminine influence in his life. He'd only been a small boy when his mother died and his father had never done anything that she knew of to fill that void in Salvatore's life. No aunts. No good friend of the family, except perhaps Therese, her father's wife.

Salvatore was only five years older than Elisa. Therese would have married Elisa's father not long after the death of Salvatore's mother.

"Did you see much of Therese growing up?" she asked as he led her up the grand staircase.

"Your father and my father are good friends and have been since before I was born."

She supposed that answered the question, except it didn't tell her how close he might have been to her stepmother. "Are you and Therese close?"

He stopped in front of a door and turned to face her. "What are you asking, *cara?*"

"Your mother died when you were little. I just wondered if…"

"Your stepmother played the role of surrogate to me?"

"Yes."

"I had no desire to have another mother."

"But you were so young."

"Old enough to know how much it hurt when Mamma died. I did not go looking for someone else to fill her place."

He'd been afraid of losing again, was perhaps still afraid of it. To love meant taking a risk, one Salvatore might never willingly submit to.

It was a depressing thought.

He pushed open the door. "This is your room."

"I don't understand why I can't stay with my father and his family."

Salvatore's brows drew together, the bronze skin between his eyes wrinkling. "You are his family, *dolcezza.*"

"Right." But not in the same way. Never in the same way. "So, why can't I stay with them?"

"You are safer here."

"I don't believe that. Your company is in charge of my father's security. I'll be safe as houses there."

"If one of the fanatics opposed to the sale of the crown jewels came looking for you, *the woman who convinced the former prince to allow her to auction them off,* would you want someone else to perhaps get in the way? Like your sister or your stepmother?"

"But he planned to sell them before I came along. It had been made public for weeks when Adamo Jewelers was chosen to host the auction. Making me a target would be senseless."

"Fanatics often are. You are willing to risk your family's safety on this belief?"

She shook her head.

He stepped back. "Your room."

"Thank you." She moved inside, her attention arrested immediately by the charming femininity of the room.

The large four-poster bed in the middle of the floor was draped with dusky mauve canopy and curtains, while the bedspread was made from fabric in a large cabbage-rose print. The drapes matched the bedspread. The dresser and vanity table were the same dark wood as the bed, but had the elegant styling of the Queen Anne era.

"It's gorgeous, but so feminine." She hadn't expected such a thing in a houseful of bachelors.

"Little has changed in this room since my mother's death."

"This was her room?"

Salvatore looked at her as if she'd gone mad. "Of course not. Can you see a Sicilian male having separate bedrooms with his wife?"

Not one in the di Vitale family. If she ever agreed to marry Salvatore, she knew the one thing they would definitely share was a bed.

"No."

"She had it decorated for female guests and the housekeeper followed this tradition when bed-coverings and such needed to be replaced."

Without her realizing it, he had come all the way into the room and now stood not two feet from her.

She stepped back a pace. "I think I'll lie down before dinner. I'm wrung out."

He reached out in a totally unexpected gesture and brushed her cheek. "Running from it will not make it go away."

"I'm not trying to make anything go away. I'm just tired."

His hand dropped from her face. "If you say so."

* * *

She was still reliving that brief touch and the gentle accusation an hour later as she moved into yet another position, hoping to get comfortable enough to sleep.

The problem was her body wanted his masculine frame curled around it. One night, and a whole year of his absence from her bed was dismissed by a body that knew what it craved, no matter how much she would like to deny it.

"You are not asleep."

She turned, a feeling of deep inevitability washing over her. He stood beside the bed, his hair ruffled from running his fingers through it, his shirt undone partway, his eyes black with an emotion all too familiar.

"What are you doing in here?"

"You cannot sleep." He set one knee on the bed. "Do not ask me how I know this, but I do. I cannot work thinking of you tossing and turning in your lonely bed."

She couldn't very well deny the tossing and turning bit. The state of the covers said all that needed to be said on that score. "I'm not lonely," she denied instead.

His hand landed beside her head on the pillow and he leaned over her, all sensual, threatening male. "Are you sure?"

CHAPTER NINE

SHE couldn't answer.

Her throat had gone dry and her lungs no longer had enough oxygen to force any words out.

His face came closer until his lips hovered less than a breath above her own. "I think, *cara mia*, that you are lonely, but this should not worry you, for I know what to do about it."

Her tongue snaked out to wet her dry lips and encountered his. She could not stop herself from taking a small taste of the masculine spice she knew to be his alone. He took it as some kind of signal and suddenly his mouth was devouring hers with carnal intensity.

His hands were everywhere. Pushing down covers. Sliding her nightgown off her. Pulling down her panties and tossing them to the floor. Tearing at his own clothes so that what buttons remained done up on his shirt popped and flew across the bed. Within seconds, they were both gloriously naked and he had her wrapped up against him just as she had craved earlier.

"You feel so good, *dolcezza*."

She lifted her hips, pressing her mound against his hardened shaft, and groaned. "So do you."

"We are meant for each other."

In this area, there could be no doubt. She might have been a virgin the first time they made love, but she knew enough to be certain the kind of passion she shared with Salvatore was rare.

She kissed the underside of his chin, then licked, loving the salty taste of his skin, the faint rasp of his five o'clock shadow. His body rippled with one long shudder.

He kissed her neck, her ear, her eyelids, the quality of the kiss changing until they were bare touches. Her eyes, which had slid shut with the first touch of his lips on her own, opened. She stared up at him.

Intense concentration masked his features.

"Salvatore?"

He kissed the very sensitive spot below her right ear. "Hmm?"

"You…" She let her voice trail off, not knowing how to voice what she was feeling, but one minute he was almost ravening with desire and the next he was being so tender, her throat felt choked with emotion.

"Shh…*dolcezza*. This time, we will take it very slowly. I will cherish every inch of you."

Which was what he did. He covered her entire body with tiny kisses, tasting her in the most erogenous spots, making her writhe with her need, but he made no effort to join his body with hers.

"Please, Salvatore, I want you."

He smiled, but he did not come up and over her. Instead he moved until his mouth was just above the now damp curls between her thighs. His head lowered and her breath sawed out in a big whoosh as deft fingers made a place for his tongue on her most sensitive flesh.

She cried out and then she just cried as he took her

from one plateau of pleasure to another, withholding the final culmination until she thought she'd go crazy with need. Then he closed his mouth down on her clitoris in the same moment two of his big fingers invaded her.

Starbursts exploded behind her eyelids as she screamed out in release. The sensation became too intense to bear and she tried to buck him off, but he kept the sensual torture going and within seconds her body was convulsing yet again in the most amazing experience of her life.

The pleasure went on and on until every muscle in her body was contracted in ecstasy, and then all at once she simply collapsed. Relaxing into the bed as boneless as melting wax.

He moved over her then, gently nudging her legs further apart to make a place for him there, where he wanted to be. The broad tip of his penis pressed inside her and she moaned with pleasure.

He lifted her knees, his muscles bulging as she did nothing to help him, and then he thrust deeply into her, his body claiming hers completely. He took his time, setting a pace that brought forth feelings she thought exhausted beyond rekindling.

He made love to her for a long time, building her arousal to another fever pitch before sending them both over the edge in mutual ecstasy.

He collapsed on top of her, his head resting so his mouth was practically touching her left ear. "Now tell me you can let me go. Tell me you will not marry me and never again feel these feelings only I can give you."

The words registered slowly as her mind began to

function on more than a sensual plane once again. Along with his words came another realization. "We did it again."

"*Sì*. Making love between we two is inevitable."

"I meant not using protection."

"*Sì.*"

"I suppose you did it on purpose again."

He rolled off her onto his back, but pulled her into his arms, cuddling her close to his side. "Can you doubt it?"

"You're ruthless when you want something."

"This is true." No denial. No attempt to justify. Simply an acceptance of this aspect to his nature.

"And you want to marry me."

"This is what I have been saying."

"Salvatore, do you believe the baby was yours?"

He was silent so long, she thought he was refusing to answer, but then his breath hitched in a strange way and she pushed herself up to see his face.

His eyes glistened suspiciously, his jaw looked hewn from granite. "*Sì*. I believe the baby I killed was my own."

She gasped, unable to accept he harbored the thought. "Salvatore, *amore*. You are so wrong. You did not kill our baby! The chances of miscarriage in the first three months are a lot higher than most people realize. The doctor told me that in the hospital. Losing the baby was not because of anything either one of us did."

"My doctor told me stress could cause miscarriage. My rejection stressed you." A single tear escaped and rolled down his temple.

He turned his head as if to hide it from her, but

she cupped his face, brushing the wetness with her thumb. "Please believe me, losing the baby was not your fault."

"This is not how I see it."

"But you are wrong!" She was shouting, but the big stubborn idiot refused to see reason.

"Actions have their consequences. I have accepted this."

"Oh, Salvatore." She didn't know what to say to make him believe her, so she just hugged him, wrapping her arms and legs around him. "It wasn't your fault. It was meant to be and neither of us could have changed it."

She'd needed to know that, that she had not done something to cause the miscarriage. "Lots of women are way more stressed than I was during that time and carry their babies to full term. You have to accept that."

"I wanted to be a father, Elisa."

Yes, she knew that now. His fury had been at believing she was pregnant with another man's child she was trying to pawn off on him, not at the prospect of fatherhood.

"Salvatore, there have not been any other men. I don't know why my father believes what he does, but you're the only lover I've ever had."

Silence met that and she waited, realizing a great deal hinged on his reaction to her words.

She might never have his love, but she had to have his respect, or there was no way she could marry him. And she realized now that not marrying him would hurt more than tying her life to a man who wanted her as desperately as he did. But if he did not believe

her, did not trust her, there was no future for them.
No matter what a pregnancy test might tell them in a
few weeks' time.

"You were a virgin?"

At least it was a question and he did not sound
incredulous at the thought.

"Yes."

"You were twenty-four."

"I know how old I was."

"This is not usual."

"I spent my childhood living with a woman who
treated sexual intimacy like cheap candy. She never
formed lasting bonds with her lovers, but I tried. I
wanted to be part of a family. I'd started school before
I finally figured out that Shawna didn't want a family.
Not even a daughter. Her lifestyle put me right off
sex. I didn't even want boys heavy petting with me
when I dated in college."

"You did not date until college?"

"Shawna sent me to an all-girls dormitory school.
Papa approved and I didn't get an opportunity to meet
boys. If I had, I would have shied away from anything
like that. I was scarred, Salvatore."

His hands were rubbing in soothing circles on her
back. "What do you mean?"

"I equated sex with the pain of being an unwanted
child, with the bitterness of loss. It wasn't until I met
you that I even felt passion for a man."

"And I demeaned you by taking what I should
have waited until after marriage to take."

She didn't want to dwell on the past. The present
and the future were what concerned her now. "Do
you believe me?"

He was talking as if he did, but she wasn't taking any chances on misreading him.

It was too important.

"*Sì*. Had I been less certain of your experience, I would have realized your innocence. There were enough clues."

"But Papa said what he did and you assumed he knew what he was talking about."

Tension filled the big body under hers. "He and I will have words."

She lifted up until their eyes met. "I think I should talk to him first."

He looked as if he wanted to dispute her words and she laid her finger across his mouth. "No. This is between him and me. Let me talk to him, all right?"

He nipped her finger and then kissed the small wound. "If that is your wish."

She appreciated the lack of argument. He might be primitive in many ways, but he wasn't a total dinosaur.

She was ready to label him a tyrannosaurus rex and be done with it three hours later.

Crossing her arms over her chest, she glared at the man she'd thought was so accommodating earlier. She felt like laughing at her naiveté. He was about as accommodating as a ten-tonne truck.

"But I don't want to go to my father's for dinner tonight."

She'd been outside on the terrace, relaxing and reading a book, trying not to think about how she and Salvatore had spent the afternoon, when he came out and dropped the bomb on her.

"I'm not even dressed for it, for heaven's sake." Wearing a pair of Espadrilles and a casual shorts outfit, she didn't feel anywhere up to dinner with her father's perfect little family.

"You can change your clothes. They are not expecting us for another forty minutes."

"I don't want to go."

"You wanted to stay in his home not so many hours ago. Why this aversion to dining with him?"

If Salvatore did not look so genuinely puzzled, she'd be ready to hit him.

"Because I'm not ready to talk to him."

Salvatore's dark eyes warmed with an understanding that undermined her determination to remain emotionally distanced from him. Not that making love with him all afternoon hadn't already done its bit to destroy that particular goal.

"I will be with you, *cara*."

"And is that supposed to make all the difference?"

Unsurprised when he frowned at her sarcasm, she turned her head away so she didn't have to see the disapproval in his expression. But not seeing didn't mean being unaware, particularly when his scent still lingered on her skin—even after a long, hot shower.

"He thinks I'm a tart."

She'd been committed to her course of action in speaking with her father and she still was, but the very need for the conversation hurt. She wanted time to mentally prepare for it.

Did other daughters have to tell their fathers they weren't floozies?

"I am convinced Francesco is working under a misapprehension." Salvatore brushed her long hair away from her face. "Perhaps he misunderstood something you said."

She looked at him, wondering if the deep vulnerability she felt was reflected in her eyes. Salvatore saw so much when it came to what she did not want him to see. "What could I have said that would make him believe I hold lovemaking cheaply?"

"I do not know, *cara,* but we will get to the bottom of this."

She didn't bother arguing the *we* in his statement. The truth was, as disparaging as she had sounded a minute ago, she was glad that in this, he was on her side.

"This is heinous, Elisa. What were you thinking to take such a risk?" Her father's expression looked like a storm on the verge of hurricane status. He'd jumped up from the chair he'd taken in the salon after greeting her and Salvatore and was pacing the floor as Salvatore told him all that had transpired over the last two days.

"I did not consider it that great a risk, for goodness' sake. The jewels were transported in secrecy. No one should have even known they were in Signor di Adamo's vault."

"You cannot keep these things quiet." A typical Sicilian male, at least six inches shorter than Salvatore with a stocky build, he glowered with all the intimidation factor of the younger man. "You should never have negotiated for Adamo Jewelers to host the auction. What would have happened, I ask you, if I had not sent Salvatore up there to watch over you?"

She made the mistake of saying, "I don't know."

His normally dark olive complexion paled. "You would be dead, or worse, child."

Fearing for his health, she got up from her seat beside Salvatore and laid her hand on her father's arm to stop his restless movements. "Calm down, Papa. I am fine and you did send Salvatore."

"Not that she wanted my interference at first."

She turned from her father to fry Salvatore with her eyes.

He lounged back on the sofa with the relaxed air of a man who had no idea how close to murder and mayhem she felt.

"You didn't listen, did you?" she asked through gritted teeth. "I hardly think it is necessary to bring it up now."

Surprisingly, Francesco laughed. "It is a good thing I sent someone so stubborn, for you are so like your mother in this!" He winked at Salvatore. "Did I not tell you? Independent like Shawna. We can only thank the good God my daughter does not share other attitudes with her mother."

Salvatore's smile froze on his face. All condescending male disappearing as comprehension dawned.

Francesco frowned. "I am sorry, Elisa. It is wrong for me to speak unkindly of your mother."

Feeling disoriented, but with dawning relief, she shook her head. "Do not worry about it. I am not blind to Shawna's belief system. She did raise me, after all."

Her father grimaced and plopped back into his chair as if he'd lost all his energy. "*Sì*. And for that I must always live with regret. Had I forced the issue, you could have grown up with the same secure home that I was able to give Annemarie, but I did not. I believed a child needed her mother." He sighed and shook his head, his forearms resting on his thighs. "Shawna filled your life with uncertainty."

Her heart felt buffeted by such revelations of regret on her father's behalf for choices made in her childhood. She stood in the middle of the room feeling as if she was in some kind of weird suspended animation.

"I don't think I would have fitted in your family with Therese on a full-time basis. I doubt she would have appreciated being expected to raise your former mistress's illegitimate daughter."

She bit her lip, realizing how bitter the words might sound, but that was not how she had meant them. It was simply the truth.

"No. You are wrong. I should have enjoyed having you as part of my family, Elisa. I wanted more children, but it was not to be." Therese, who had entered the room quietly, went to stand by Salvatore's chair, her expression serene as usual. "Annemarie would have enjoyed living with her older sister full-time. She will be sorry she missed this visit, but she will not return from her trip with friends in the country for several days."

This was simply too much. Elisa loved her younger sister, but they were so different and she was not at all convinced Annemarie could care one way or the other if she missed a visit from her infrequently seen older sister. "We are not close."

"You could have been, if things had been different.'' This from her father, who looked ready to immerse himself in a full-fledged guilt attack.

And no doubt he would be happier if she were more amenable, like her half-sister, but she was twenty-five years old. The time for such considerations was long past.

"It's a bit late for such thoughts."

Francesco winced and she clenched her hands at her sides.

"I don't mean that in a negative way. I meant you are not doing yourself any favors focusing on something that is over and done with."

Therese laid her hand on Francesco's shoulder. "She is right, *amore*. You have been too caught up in memories since your heart episode, but these considerations do no one any good. What is past is past. We must live in the present and we have your daughter with us now. You should enjoy her visit, not waste it mourning over old regrets."

Francesco's face filled with love for his wife of twenty-three years. "*Sì, bella mia,* as always, you are right."

Therese's still beautiful cheeks turned a soft pink and she squeezed Francesco's shoulder. "You! Sweet talk will not get you canoli for dinner. You heard the doctor with ears that work as good as mine."

They continued their gentle banter through the meal, but afterward Francesco's good humor vanished when Salvatore informed him he had no intention of leaving Elisa to stay in the Guiliano home.

"Your father is in America and your grandfather has gone on that cruise of the Greek islands with the widow Genose. It is not seemly for my daughter to stay alone with you.''

Elisa felt like laughing. She could understand the concern were she Annemarie, but she'd been living on her own for years. However, she said nothing. Let Salvatore fight his own battles. The whole living-arrangement thing had been his idea.

''That is precisely why we are staying at my home and not here. Until the auction is over, Elisa is at risk. Whoever she is with is also at risk. I can watch over her more effectively if my attention is not divided with the risks posed to those around her as well.''

Her father looked much less impressed by this argument than Elisa had been. His eyes narrowed and his chest puffed up with male pride. ''I can watch over my family just fine. Your own company has ensured that the security in my home is top-of-the-line.''

''Nevertheless, Elisa will stay with me.'' Salvatore, who had persuaded Signor di Adamo with perfect finesse, faced Francesco with primitive male aggression and not one attempt at conciliation.

Therese shook her head and clicked her tongue. ''Ah, an argument between two stubborn, proud males is not my idea of after-dinner entertainment.'' She turned to Elisa. ''Come, child, we will go out to the garden and I will show you my new Pink Butterfly orchid. I planted it soon after your visit last year. It is just now in bloom.''

Elisa didn't understand why Salvatore wasn't trying harder to handle her father more carefully, but she had no intention of letting him and her father make any more decisions regarding her life. ''I'd love to see your orchids but first...'' She turned to her father.

"I agree with Salvatore. I will not put you and Therese at risk. I'll go off on my own first."

Her father opened his mouth to speak, but Salvatore forestalled him. "That is not going to happen."

She didn't bother to argue, simply lifted her brow as if to ask, Is it not?, and left the room with Therese.

Salvatore and her father joined them outside a few minutes later. Francesco had the look of a man whose favorite sports team had won an important tournament. "It is a beautiful evening, is it not? The fragrance of flowers, the warm air, the company of good people."

Once again the expansive Italian host, he beamed at the others.

Therese smiled. "You two have worked out your difference of opinion, *sì?*"

"*Sì.*" With what Elisa considered an extreme lack of subtlety on his part, he leaned to whisper something in Therese's ear.

She smiled too as he spoke.

"It is time to go, *cara.*" Salvatore slid his arm around her in a way that blatantly claimed possession.

Shocked, she stiffened against him, but he pulled her close to his side and kept her there through their goodbyes.

Her father didn't act surprised, though, and Therese had the look of an Italian woman making wedding plans in her mind. Elisa felt as if she'd been measured for the wedding gown and eyed for the cut of the veil by the time Salvatore tucked her into the passenger seat of his car to take her home.

*   *   *

Salvatore waited for the inquisition to start. Elisa had been ominously silent since he and her father had rejoined the women in the garden.

She was too smart not to realize that certain things had been said between him and Francesco. The older man's smug acceptance of the situation gave that away. Not that he had easily been convinced of the rightness of Elisa staying with Salvatore. Even after he promised her father he intended to marry her, Francesco had balked.

But Salvatore had refused to budge and he had reminded Francesco just how independent his daughter was. Her threat to go off on her own was not an idle one. Neither man wanted that to happen. Commenting that the world was a different place from when he had courted Therese, Francesco had finally agreed to Salvatore taking Elisa back to his home.

Elisa shifted in her seat until he could feel the weight of her beautiful green gaze on him. "What did you tell my father to bring such an about-face?"

"I told him the truth."

"Which part of the truth?" she pressed.

"That I intend to marry you."

No gasp of outrage was forthcoming. "Is that all?"

He could tell nothing of what she was thinking from the bland tone in her voice.

"Not precisely, but it is all you need to know."

When Francesco had pressed for a promise Salvatore would not take advantage of his daughter, Salvatore had made the commitment with a clear conscience. Making love to her was not taking advantage. It was absolutely necessary, both to his campaign to convince her to agree to marriage and to both their well-being. She might be unwilling to admit it, but she needed him every bit as much as he needed her.

"I see."

Nothing. He stood the silence for a full five minutes of monotonous driving before breaking it. "I do intend to marry you."

"You've said so."

He cursed under his breath. "*Sì.* I have."

It was her own intentions in the matter that were in question. He fully expected to have his way, but he wanted her acceptance. He wanted her to admit that life without him would not be an option, regardless that she had spent the last year pretending it was.

"And that was enough to convince Papa my virtue would not be compromised by staying alone with a single man?"

At the mention of her virtue, Salvatore's grip tightened on the steering wheel and the discussion of their future took a back seat for the time being. *"Mi dispiace."*

"What are you sorry for?" She sounded only mildly interested, but he was not fooled.

Her own hands were clasped in her lap with white-knuckle intensity.

"I misunderstood your father, and because of it I caused both you and myself untold grief."

"Didn't it occur to you, even once, my father was not implying my moral values when he said I was like Shawna?"

"To my shame, no."

"Why?" The bewilderment in her voice tore at his

heart. "Did I do something to make you believe that?"

"No."

"I don't understand."

He hated admitting what drove him, but she deserved the truth. "I wanted you."

"Yes, that has been well and truly established."

"I could not have you if I believed you to be a virgin."

"Because you were not thinking marriage."

"*Sì.*" Anger and disgust with himself made his teeth grind together.

He had been considering marriage a year ago, but not with her. He had not wanted the volatile feelings he associated with his humiliation at Sofia's hand to be part of his married life and Elisa elicited the most violent of feelings in him. Both passion and possession.

"So you convinced yourself I was a well-used cherry tree, ripe for the picking."

He winced at the analogy, but nodded, a short, sharp movement of his head.

"Because of Sofia?"

"Because of my own stubborn pride, all right?" He hated this kind of talk. Acknowledging emotions was bad enough. Discussing them was torture.

"All right."

Again the silence.

He kept expecting her to push for more. Did not women always want to dissect the emotions of a situation until they were laid bare in every way for their edification?

Yet, she said nothing.

They arrived back at the house. He helped her from the car and she thanked him, but she did not re-open the conversation.

That bothered him. It was as if it was not important enough to her to pursue.

Heaven knew he did not want to discuss his feelings, but still he felt cheated. She should want to.

If she cared about him.

She had not repeated any declarations of love since their reunion. Perhaps all tender feelings for him were gone, but she did not respond in his arms like a woman who felt nothing more than sexual gratification.

What they shared when their bodies joined was sacred.

Perhaps she was attempting to distance herself from him again. Go back to that place she had been for the last year where she had not needed him, had in fact wanted nothing to do with him. He was not about to let that happen.

He led her into the house, but did not give her the chance to go to her own room.

He simply swung her into his arms and carried her up the stairs.

She looped her arms lightly around his neck, her expression too indecipherable for his liking. ''Where are you taking me?''

''To bed.''

''Whose?''

''Mine.''

''Do I have any say in the matter?''

Tension gripped him. ''Do you want to sleep alone?''

He waited for what felt like hours, but was more likely only a few seconds before she let out a small puff of air and tucked her head into the curve of his neck.

"No."

CHAPTER TEN

SALVATORE let out the breath he had been holding and carried her into his bedroom. Relief pulsed through him. He could not press her if she truly did not want to share his bed and yet he had no idea how he would have handled her rejection.

He did not bother to turn on any lights. He wanted this time together to be elemental...without distractions.

He couldn't be slow this time. His need was too great. Stripping her, he touched each soft curve with voracious need to elicit her complete surrender. She urged him on with moans and little feminine cries that increased his own ardor to frightening proportions.

He brushed the damp curls at the apex of her thighs. ''I want you, Elisa.''

She widened her legs, letting his fingers dip into the heated honey waiting for him. He caressed the swollen flesh he found there, the small, swollen button that he knew brought her extreme pleasure.

Arching toward his hand, she panted. She moaned. She writhed, her legs moving restlessly as he circled her clitoris with his thumb.

''I want you too.''

''Enough to take me for a lifetime?''

''Don't tease!''

He was seriously tempted to push it, to gain her acquiescence to his proposal by whatever means, fair or foul, at his disposal, but in the end, he had no more control than she did. He needed her.

He rolled onto his back, pulling her with him. "If you want me, take me."

He would at least have the satisfaction of knowing the seduction was mutual.

She didn't hesitate. She mounted him, opening herself over his hard shaft and pressing downward until she enveloped him completely. Her swollen inner tissues clamped tight around him, caressing his shaft in small muscular contractions.

He groaned and thrust upward, his hands tight on her thighs.

Her head fell back and her long hair cascaded down her spine. He could not see her expression in the semi-darkness of the room, but her posture was that of a woman in the throes of sexual abandon.

"You feel so good inside of me. It's as if we aren't two people any more."

Could she hear what she was saying? They were one. She must realize they belonged together. And then all conscious thought flew from his head as she rode him to mind-numbing pleasure and a climax that left his body shaking beneath hers.

She fell against his chest, her own cries ringing in his ears.

Elisa didn't know how long she lay in a boneless mass on Salvatore's chest, but eventually she lifted herself off.

He refused to let her get far and pulled her against him, his strong arms comforting and warm bands around her.

She snuggled into his side, feeling replete and

physically sated. Only it was much more than that. She felt an emotional well-being that she had thought she would never experience with him again.

"Salvatore?"

"Hmm?" His hand played idly over her ribs, his own body only having just relaxed from its shuddering reaction to their lovemaking.

"How come it's OK for you to make love to me on this trip to Sicily, but the last time I was down, it would have been a dishonor to my family if you had seduced me?"

His hand stilled.

"Is it because I'm not staying in my father's house?" That would help explain his intractability on the subject.

Surprisingly, he shook his head.

"Is it because you told my father you intended to marry me?"

"No."

She didn't think so. Somehow, she couldn't convince herself that her father would be a modern sort who thought it was OK for his daughter to shack up with her intended. "Then why?"

"Because, *amore,* in my mind, you have been my wife since the night you told me about the baby."

She sucked in air like a boxer trying not to go down.

"You're kidding." Not original, but her brain had frozen on that amazing statement.

"Marriage is no mocking matter to me."

She swallowed the disbelief trying to choke her. "If you're serious then I guess that makes you pretty poor husband material."

She was only half kidding.

He flipped her on her back and loomed over her, all domineering male, but she didn't feel dominated. He would never hurt her physically and she was beginning to see that the emotional wounds he had dealt her pained his conscience as much as her heart.

"What do you mean by that?" he demanded.

"Well, if you've been married for the last year to me in your mind, that makes you an unfaithful husband, doesn't it?" She wanted to be flippant, but her words came out very serious and too vulnerable for her comfort.

The idea of him making love to another woman, probably one who was way more sophisticated and experienced than she was caused a sharp pain in the region of her heart.

"Why would you say this?"

"Oh, please." He was so oversexed, they could write manuals on him. "You're not exactly the celibate type, Salvatore." And the thought he'd gone an entire year without sex at all was laughable.

"Nevertheless, I have been celibate." His tone of voice dared her to disbelieve him.

Her breath sort of froze in her windpipe. She shook her head, unable to get words out.

"*Sì.* I had desire for only one woman and she avoided me with the professionalism of a tax evader."

It was unbelievable. Impossible. Salvatore had had no one for a whole year? "Is that the truth?"

"I will never lie to you."

She looked through the dimness, trying to read the expression in his almost black eyes. Even the darkness could not hide the sincerity burning there. She believed him.

"What would you have done if I had found someone else?"

"You would not. You belonged to me even when you wanted to deny it."

"But what if I had?" she pushed.

"It did not happen." And the overwhelming fury she sensed in him made her very glad it had not.

Then he turned his head and light coming in through the door exposed a stark pain she could not bear to see.

She cupped his cheek. "No. It did not happen. I didn't want it to."

He nodded. "See? You knew deep beneath your anger and disappointment in me that we belonged together."

He did not love her, had made no excuses for that, but such a description of their relationship was not something to be scoffed at.

"So, I guess you're pretty disappointed with the kind of wife I've been for the past year." Part of her still needed to make a joke of his incredible statement.

He didn't laugh. He didn't even smile. "You have been hurting. I knew this. I wanted to make it better, but did not know how."

"It helps to know you believe me about our baby, that you grieve its death as much as I do." The words came out sounding more like a question than a statement of fact.

He kissed her forehead, his lips tender enough to make her smile despite remembered grief. "I do believe you and I do grieve. This grief is another thing that draws us together, something we share that no one else is party to.''

She considered that and his assertion earlier that the doctor had said making another baby might be beneficial for her mental health. "You made love to me again without protection.''

"I did not.''

Feeling the extra wetness between her legs, she shook her head. "There is physical evidence to the contrary.''

"It was you who made love to me this time.''

Remembering her wild ride and how she had exulted in bringing them both such pleasure, she flushed with stirrings of resurging desire. "So this time it is my fault?''

"It is mutual. It has always been mutual.'' It was his turn to sound as if he needed confirmation of that fact.

He'd promised not to lie to her. She could give him no less than the truth herself. "Yes.''

"Say you will marry me.''

"Because you feel guilty about the loss of our child?'' She couldn't help feeling that was still a big part of his desire to get married.

"Because I do not wish to face a future without you.''

Again his tone dared a denial. She didn't want to give one. She wanted to believe him. He might not love her, but he needed her and heaven knew…she needed him. She'd only been half-alive over the past year.

"Yes.''

The heartbeat beneath her hand sped up and

Salvatore stretched out his hand to turn on the bedside light.

She blinked against the unexpected brightness.

A vibrantly triumphant male loomed above her, taking up her entire vision. "Say that again."

"Yes, I will marry you."

She got only a moment of seeing a grin that indicated he was really happy before his lips covered hers and he took her on a sensual journey that outdid anything she had ever experienced with him before.

The next few days flew by in a whirl of activity. Not only did Elisa have to finish plans for the auction, but she also now had her stepmother calling every fifteen minutes with suggestions for her upcoming wedding.

Therese had been disappointed to learn the event was scheduled for two weeks hence, saying a proper wedding could not be planned in under six months. Francesco had argued that he wanted to give his daughter a traditional Sicilian wedding, but both Elisa and Salvatore had remained adamant.

She wasn't sure why Salvatore felt the need to do the deed so quickly, but she knew her own motives.

She couldn't help feeling they had made a baby that first night back together. While Salvatore might consider them already man and wife, she wanted the legal ties as well if she was going to carry his child again.

Everything this time around was going to be right.

So, although it meant putting together a wedding and an auction at the same time, she did not complain.

"How did Shawna take the news of our upcoming marriage?"

Elisa looked up from the guest list for the auction. Salvatore had given her the library to work in, bringing in all the equipment she required to finish organizing the auction. A fax machine, a computer with high-speed internet service, a phone with two lines—whatever she wanted, she got.

She smiled at the man who acted as if nothing was too good for her. ''My mother isn't keen on the institution of marriage, you know.''

He nodded, the glow of satisfaction he'd worn since her agreement to become his wife not dimming an iota. Shawna's lack of approval would mean very little to him.

''She wished me well and said perhaps marriage was the best way to spend my twenties.'' She'd also said that a woman didn't really come into her own until after forty and Elisa could evaluate her life and arcane commitments then.

Sharing that sentiment with Salvatore was not on the agenda, particularly since she had no such intention. This marriage was for life, and if she thought Salvatore felt any differently about it she would never have agreed to marry him.

''Is she flying over for the wedding?''

''No. She's working and can't spare the time.'' Strangely, that had not bothered Elisa.

She'd finally come to accept that her mother's lack of affection was not her fault, but a deficiency in the older woman's emotional makeup.

Salvatore laid his hand on Elisa's shoulder. ''Are you OK with this?''

''I'm fine. Shawna was not a woman who should have had children.''

"I can only be grateful she did not realize this until after you were born, *cara*."

Warmth suffused Elisa's heart and she leaned into Salvatore's body. "I'm almost done with the guest list for the auction."

"I will need it to run a background check on all those attending."

"Signor di Adamo cannot afford that level of security."

Salvatore looked at her as if she'd lost her mind. "It matters not what he can afford. This is your safety and I will not have it compromised."

"In other words, you aren't charging him."

"You are mine. I protect what is mine."

"Did you ever wonder if you were born in the right millennium? You're a total dinosaur when it comes to relationships."

An expression she could not decipher entered his eyes. "Surely, it is not that bad?"

He really seemed to care so she let him off the hook. "It's fine. If I thought you were walking on me, I'd let you know."

"It is true. You are not shy in voicing your opinion."

She grinned at the irritation in his voice. "I'm also not in danger. We've hired a top-notch auctioneer and two of your operatives will be responsible for the crown jewels' display. My role will be a background one in every way. If anything, Signor di Adamo will be in the limelight, not me."

Salvatore just looked at her, his face set in granite-hard contours.

She rolled her eyes. "Fine. I'll give you the list. I don't even know why I bothered arguing."

Salvatore had given her complete reign regarding the auction plans, but he had been intractable on the issue of her security from day one.

"Is Adamo Jewelers ready for business again?"

"*Sì.* Your boss is happy with his new security."

"I'm sure he is." She'd spoken to Signor di Adamo, but their conversation had centered on the upcoming auction.

The old man was very excited about the influx of capital their fee for hosting the auction would give the store.

She ticked an item off her list and then looked up again. "Salvatore?"

"*Sì?*"

"Milan is too far away for me to commute to work."

His expression turned wary. "This is true."

"I don't like leaving my boss in the lurch. He's depended a lot on me over the past few years. It would break my heart if he lost the store after all this because he didn't have the manpower to run it."

She didn't know what the answer was. Salvatore could not transfer his office from Milan. She wasn't even sure she wanted to go on working after the baby was born. She wanted to be a mother first and foremost. Her passion for gemology was secondary for the time being.

But the thought of Signor di Adamo relying on her and her not fulfilling her obligation to him left a hollow place in her tummy.

Salvatore's silence clued her in that something was

not right. She examined his face. The wariness was even more apparent in his dark eyes, but his mouth was set in a grim line—as if he was prepared for some kind of argument.

"What's wrong?"

"Nothing is *wrong*."

She narrowed her eyes, trying to interpret the nuances of his expression and tone. "What aren't you telling me?"

His spine stiffened and his expression went even more stone-like. "I procured a new assistant for Signor di Adamo."

"You what?" Startled, she stared at him. "When?"

Looking as uncomfortable as an overly confident, gorgeous Sicilian male could look, Salvatore gave a minimal shrug. "I began the search for candidates the day we returned to Sicily."

Perhaps she should be angry, but she knew this man too well to be truly shocked by what he had done. It had been his intention all along to marry her and he knew her boss's dilemma weighed heavily on her. He was just taking care of all possible obstacles to the path he wanted to pursue.

"Signor di Adamo said nothing about it."

"I asked him not to," Salvatore said, with the air of a man intent on confessing it all.

"I see."

She looked back to her paperwork and made a note about a question she wanted to ask the caterer. Then she pulled out her notebook she was using to organize details for the wedding and put a similar question on the caterer's page.

"You could not work at Adamo Jewelers and live in Milan."

"True." She clicked into her e-mail program on the computer and downloaded her mail.

There were three more replies that she took note of before skimming a message from Therese regarding flowers at the wedding.

"It would be an impossible situation. Surely you must see that."

"Impossible situation. Yes." She wasn't really paying close attention because it suddenly struck her that she wanted a traditional, over-the-top wedding gown and she didn't know if she could get one on such short notice. "I bet Shawna would know someone," she muttered as she pulled up the address file for her mother's entourage.

She would call Shawna's secretary. The woman knew every fashion designer in New York on a first-name basis.

"You have no reason to be angry with me."

"Angry?" She picked up the phone to dial the secretary, but then realized the timing was wrong and put it back down.

Making a quick note to call later, she went back to her work.

"A pregnant woman should not be working in such a dangerous environment. You were shot at."

The urgency in Salvatore's voice finally got through the haze of thoughts competing for her attention and she let her gaze lift to him. "What?"

Dark chocolate eyes snapped with determination. "It is for the best."

"What is for the best?" Had she missed something here?

"Signor di Adamo taking on a new assistant."

"Did I say it wasn't?"

"You could not continue after our marriage. It would not be practical."

"I agree."

Rather than soothe him, her acquiescence seemed to spur him on to more arguments in favor of what he had done. "You are no doubt pregnant with my child. Suppose you were shot at again. The stress would be too much for you."

"You're really worried about the stress thing and my being pregnant, aren't you?"

"It is a concern, *sì*."

"Salvatore, have I somehow implied I was unhappy about you going to the effort to find my boss someone to replace me?"

"No, but you are too independent and no doubt see it as overstepping bounds on my part."

"I haven't said so, have I?"

"No."

"You did it because you knew you were going to marry me, no matter what, didn't you?"

"*Sì.*"

"It never occurred to you that I might stand firm in my refusal?"

His sheer confidence amazed her even as she found it somewhat comforting.

"No. And you probably find that arrogant on my part."

"Well, yes, but I don't mind."

"You do not?"

"No."

"You are not upset about the assistant."

He said it as a statement, but she answered anyway. "No. You wanted me to be comfortable leaving Signor di Adamo and I appreciate that."

"You do?" He looked and sounded shocked.

She laughed. "I'm not that independent."

"Excuse me, but you are."

Laughing again, she shook her head. "Maybe I am changing."

She wanted the ties of family and that meant allowing a certain amount of interdependence. Not that she had a hope of remaining independent of Salvatore anyway. She needed him on a fundamental level that made her more vulnerable than she had ever been, even with her parents. It scared her a little, but she was learning to accept the feelings he evoked in her.

"And this change allows you to rely on me?"

"Uh-huh."

He leaned down and kissed her hard and slow and deep. She was a puddle of sensation when he stood up. "I like this change."

She was too muddled by his kiss to answer.

Annemarie came home early from her trip to help with wedding preparations. The three women were in a war conference around the dining-room table when Salvatore and Francesco came in two nights later.

Salvatore leaned down and kissed her full on the mouth, making Therese smile and Annemarie blush. "All is arranged for the security of the auction."

"I do not understand why you must attend.

Everything has been seen to already.'' Francesco frowned at Elisa.

She gritted her teeth. She'd wanted this closer relationship but she was learning it had both benefits and drawbacks. ''I am in charge of the auction. I cannot let Signor di Adamo down.''

''He has a new assistant.''

''Who knows nothing about putting on an event of this magnitude.'' She'd gotten something from her years of being Shawna Tyler's daughter. ''I will be fine. Salvatore will be there watching over me.''

Francesco turned on his future son-in-law. ''Why can you not speak sense into this daughter of mine?''

''I have tried,'' Salvatore ruefully confessed, ''and failed.''

''Do you really think I'm going to spend my entire married life letting Salvatore dictate to me?'' she asked the room in general, but with a pointed look at her father.

''This I cannot imagine,'' Therese remarked with a smile.

''You are so strong, so self-sufficient.'' Annemarie's expression said she wasn't sure if that was a good or a bad thing.

Elisa closed her notebook and slipped her pen in its pocket. ''I don't believe a woman's intellect or common sense is inferior to a man's, that is all.''

Francesco walked around the table and patted Annemarie's shoulder. ''You are my Sicilian kitten and your sister is my little American tigress. Each of you has a beauty inherent to your nature, though they are very different. A father could not ask for better daughters than mine.''

Annemarie blushed again and Elisa felt heat climbing up her own cheeks. "I'm not exactly a tigress."

Salvatore's eyes heated with reminders of how they spent their nights. "Are you not, *cara?*"

She couldn't begin to answer the message in his expression in front of her father and she glared at him for making her think inappropriate thoughts that had her blushing as fiercely as her shy sister.

Her father did not miss the byplay and slapped his thigh, chuckling. "Elisa is a good match for you, eh, Salvatore? Her sass, it warms the blood, no?" He winked at the younger man and then turned his attention to Therese. "Can you imagine a year ago this man believed he would be happy married to our kitten? He would have overwhelmed her a week into the courtship, but my Elisa...she will give Salvatore a run for his money, no?"

Francesco laughed uproariously at his own joke while Therese smiled and Annemarie blushed, but Elisa was confused.

"He wanted to marry Annemarie?" She looked at her younger sister, who shrugged, looking very uncomfortable being the center of the conversation.

"It was something I considered. That is all." Salvatore's expression revealed nothing of his thoughts.

"*Sì.* He spoke of it to me during your visit here last summer."

It was positively arcane, what her father was implying, that he and Salvatore had discussed marriage between him and Annemarie without her knowledge.

"While I was here?" she parroted, grasping immediately on to the fact that meant Salvatore had been considering marriage to the perfect, virginal sister while using flirtation to seduce the one he believed to be a tart.

"I sensed a rapport between you two that made me wonder at his choice of my daughters, but I said nothing. A man cannot interfere with young love."

"Love had nothing to do with it," she said, pain blossoming in her heart like a poisonous flower.

"Of course, the feelings, they come with time, but still, I was right. The attraction between you two bore fruit."

More fruit than her father would ever know about.

A baby that had been lost and a relationship that would never be the same.

She turned to Salvatore, feeling a yawning pit growing inside her. "You spoke to my father about marriage to Annemarie last summer?"

She needed confirmation, to hear from his own lips that he had been thinking of marriage to her sister while contemplating her own seduction.

"*Sì*, but it was nothing."

She wondered how he defined nothing. To her this revelation was something powerful, something painful.

She didn't believe he could be so cavalier about it, as if it did not matter. Didn't he realize how ugly such a circumstance made everything? It denigrated her to the level of bimbo for a short affair, but then when had she convinced herself what they had shared before had been anything else for him? Had she not gotten pregnant with his child, he would have broken up with her and married her sister.

She had to lock her jaw to hold back the cry of pain that thought evoked.

Salvatore was no longer smiling. "As your father has said, nothing came of it."

"*Sì*. I knew it would not and I was right."

Annemarie continued to look incredibly embarrassed while her father was so tied up in his typical male pride in being right that he had not caught on to the fact his disclosures were less than pleasing to either daughter's ears. And if Elisa controlled herself, he never would. This wasn't something she wanted made the subject of a family discussion.

"Obviously." Therese sighed, but smiled. "You do not need to crow about it, Francesco. We can all see for ourselves how right you were."

Elisa forced herself to laugh along with the others and managed not to flinch away when Salvatore touched her to help her from her chair and lead her out to the patio for before-dinner drinks. And somehow she kept up the pretense of happy bride-to-be for the rest of the evening, her heart as good as dead in her chest.

CHAPTER ELEVEN

THE minute they got home, Elisa peeled away from Salvatore and headed for the stairs. "I'm sleeping on my own tonight."

"Che cosa?"

She paused in her headlong flight up the stairs and turned her head so she could glare at him. "You heard me. I don't want to sleep with you."

"What is the matter with you?"

That perfectly gorgeous face was set in lines of genuine puzzlement and that made her even angrier. How could he not know what was wrong? Was he that insensitive?

"I'm not sleeping with a man who thought I was good enough to screw, but not good enough to marry!"

He gasped. "Do not speak like that of yourself!"

"You're allowed to think it, but I'm not allowed to say it? Get real, Salvatore."

He looked completely taken aback by her words. "I do not think this thing."

"Yes, you do, and don't you bother denying it." The tears were burning her throat and eyes, but she would have her say and get to the privacy of the guest room before she let them fall. "You spoke to my father about marrying Annemarie while you were busy flirting with me and seducing me, and why did you do that?"

169

"Because—"

She didn't let him finish. "You thought I was a slut you could sleep with and leave, but you had no intention of having any sort of future with me."

"Perhaps I tried to convince myself of that, but—"

"But nothing! I can't believe you think I'll go to bed with you after finding this out. You're only marrying me out of misplaced guilt. If I hadn't had the bad luck to get pregnant the first time, you would be married to Annemarie by now."

A sort of dawning horror was reflected in his eyes. He was probably appalled she knew the truth. "You cannot believe this."

"Don't insult my intelligence by trying to tell me otherwise. I may have acted like one with you, Salvatore, but I'm not a fool."

Did he think she couldn't put two and two together? With that she spun on her heel and rushed up the stairs.

He shouted her name, cursed in Italian and then yelled at her to be careful. She ignored all of it and slammed into the guest room, locking the door and then falling against it as she let the burning tears track down her cheeks.

Seconds later he pounded on the door, making it reverberate against her. "Elisa, let me in."

"N-no."

"Be reasonable. Open up."

"I—I w-won't."

The pounding stopped. "Are you crying, *amore?*"

"Wh-what d-do you c-care?" she choked out between deep, gasping sobs.

It hurt so much.

She felt used.

She felt betrayed.

And she felt scared.

Because she was sure she was pregnant with the baby of a man who could think so little of her that he could plan to seduce her while courting her sister for marriage.

"I care. Please, *cara,* open the door."

The unaccustomed pleading had no effect on her. She was in too much emotional pain.

"G-go away!"

"I cannot do that."

"Then I w-will." She pushed herself away from the door and trudged across the floor to the *en suite*.

Her body shook with crying, her stomach hurt and she couldn't breathe through her nose, much less see a clear path through her tears. Disoriented, she bumped into the doorjamb on her way into the bathroom. Stumbling back, she cried harder.

She finally made it into the bathroom and shut that door as well. She also locked it. The extra layer of wood between them muffled Salvatore's voice, but it did not obliterate it. She turned on the shower, climbed in the stall fully clothed and sat on the floor, letting the hot water cover her while she cried out her grief.

She hadn't cried after the baby died. She'd had no one to share her grief and somehow that had made it impossible for her to express it, but now the tears came. She let the pain of its loss wash over her right along with the agony of this fresh betrayal by Salvatore.

He was a cold-hearted snake. How could she have forgotten that fact?

He didn't want her. He wanted Annemarie. The shy kitten. Perfect wife material for a traditional Sicilian male.

The physical ache inside her grew until she turned onto her side on the floor of the shower stall, curled up like an infant. She tried to hold it in, this pain that splintered through her, shredding her heart, her very soul, but it would not be contained.

Once released, she could not contain her grief. It was all mixed up inside her, tonight's revelations and her miscarriage. Feelings she had been denying for a year washed over her drowning her in their sorrow. Tears poured out of her while her muscles cramped in physical response to her mental agony.

"Santo cielo!" Strong hands curved around her shoulders, pulling her toward a big male body. "Elisa, do not do this to yourself."

"I hate you, Salvatore. You hurt me." She said more muddled things, few of which even she understood. Most of which had nothing to do with her father's revelations.

He didn't respond with words, but picked her up, taking her from the shower, and turned off the water. She tried to fight him, but her grief drained her and she ended up lying against him like a soggy, acquiescent child.

He stripped her and dried her off, all the while remonstrating with her for getting into such a state. She ignored him, crying silently, but still crying.

He groaned when he touched her face and brushed away tears, only to watch as her cheeks became drenched again. "*Cara,* please, *dolcezza,* you will make yourself sick."

She shook her head, trying to shut out his presence.

He wrapped a fluffy bath sheet around her and then set her on the closed toilet seat. "What can I say to make it better?"

"Nothing. I want to go to bed. To sleep. Alone." She glared at him with wet eyes. "Without you," she said for emphasis in case he didn't get it.

He sighed and pulled off his wet clothes. He toweled his hair and she realized he'd gotten pretty soaked taking her from the shower. "I cannot leave you like this."

"Because my feelings don't matter to you."

"This is not true." He tightened his jaw like a man trying to hold in his temper.

"It is true. I want to be alone and you won't let me. Wh-what d-do you c-call that?" She'd started crying harder again.

He jerked around and marched out of the bathroom, through a door she now saw was hanging in a broken doorframe. So that was how he'd gotten in. Brute force. At least he had left. She could wallow in her pain in peace now.

It was too much of an effort to get up and go into the bedroom, so she sat on the toilet seat and let the tears fall.

That was how he found her when he returned a few minutes later. He swept her into his arms and carried her through to the bedroom. He laid her on the bed as if she were some kind of fragile porcelain doll. Then he tucked the covers around her, but he made no move to join her.

And that was what she wanted. It was.

She needed to be away from him to think.

He sat beside her and she shied away from him. She couldn't help it, but he scowled.

"I won't hurt you, damn it."

"You already have." She said it in such a defeated tone, she shocked herself.

His complexion went from olive darkness to paste white in a breath. "It was not my intention."

"That doesn't make it better." She wasn't even sure if she was talking about now or a year ago, but it didn't really matter. The pain was now. The grief was now.

She went to turn away from him, but he lifted her into a sitting position and pressed a wine glass to her lips.

She refused to drink. "What is it?"

"Just wine. You need something to settle you."

"Alcohol is bad for the baby."

"Your tears and upset are worse for the baby than a few sips of wine."

She knew he was right and guilt assailed her.

Her self-indulgence could very well be putting their baby at risk. She sipped the wine and reined in her emotions.

She'd stopped crying. Salvatore had handed her a tissue to mop up and now they both sat in silence. Her under the covers, him on top, the distance between them as good as a mile.

"I want to sleep alone."

He nodded. "If that is your wish."

And he left.

And she wondered if it really had been. Her emotions were careening all over the place and she hated this seesaw they seemed to be on.

She turned on her side, away from the mental image of Salvatore sitting beside her on the bed, and tried to sleep. In sleep, the pain would go away.

Salvatore went downstairs to the library. He pulled out a bottle of aged Scotch from the cabinet below one of the mahogany bookcases and poured himself a glass. He sipped, but tasted nothing. He wanted more than anything to go back up to that bedroom and convince Elisa that she was wrong about his feelings for her, wrong about his motives.

He wouldn't. He couldn't. He'd left in the first place because she looked so fragile, so ready to go over the edge of her emotional control once again. Like Elisa, he had now accepted she was pregnant even without the confirmation of a test. He could not force a confrontation that would put the baby at risk. Not again. He would not allow his stupidity to end in the death of his child again.

He slumped into the armchair closest to where Elisa had set up her temporary office, feeling as if the very heart had been ripped from his chest.

The pain he had known upon discovering Sofia's betrayal was like a pinprick compared to the slashing knife wound to his soul inflicted by Elisa's rejection.

It had only been as he sat there, forced to witness an emotional pain so profound it pounded his heart like a sledgehammer that he had realized the true extent of his feelings for her. He loved her.

Why did that come as such a shock?

No other emotion could explain how completely

necessary she was to him. He had existed, not lived, the past year while she had avoided him.

And, like an idiot he had denied the emotion, preferring to believe he was righting a wrong done. Admitting he had been prompted by love would have given her too much power over him. So he had protected his vulnerability, only to destroy his chance at happiness with the one woman that mattered.

She believed he had thought she was not as good as Annemarie. *Porca miseria!* She could believe he still felt that way, for all he knew.

The conversation he had had with Francesco had been so short, of so little consequence, he had allowed himself to forget it. It had happened two days after Elisa's arrival in Sicily. He too was visiting his family home and had already spent one evening and an afternoon in her company.

His response to her had been so strong that he had reacted by going to Francesco and casually mentioning the idea of marriage between himself and Annemarie. Anything to avoid being controlled by the violence of feeling Elisa provoked in him. Francesco had shrugged and said he would not be adverse to joining their two families, but that had been the extent of it.

Salvatore had never once attempted to court Annemarie, but he doubted that would make any difference to Elisa. Not in her current state, definitely. She had reacted like a woman betrayed and he did not blame her.

His own stupidity had led to such a pass.

She hated him when he had finally come to the

realization that he loved her and needed her more than he needed life-giving sustenance.

He tossed back the Scotch and poured himself another glass.

Elisa tossed in the bed, the covers twisting around her legs, and fought the memory of Salvatore's face when she had sent him away. He had looked devastated.

Why?

OK, so she was probably pregnant with his baby. He no doubt didn't want her tearing off to parts unknown again, but she hadn't threatened to do that. She hadn't even said she wanted to call off the wedding. As much as she hurt, she could not quite make those words come out of her mouth.

They were too permanent.

A lifetime without him elicited more fear and pain than the knowledge that he had thought so little of her last summer.

Last summer. Those two words blinked like a caution light at a four-way stop in her mind. She'd been reacting as if this revelation was about something recent, *something now*. Only it wasn't.

Salvatore had told her why he'd thought such stupid things about her. Because of a misunderstanding over something her father had said. And what had Salvatore said about that, besides a very uncharacteristic apology? Oh, yes…that he had wanted her so much he had needed to believe she wasn't a virgin so he could have her.

Because he hadn't been thinking marriage.

He was thinking it now, though, and according to him he'd been married to her in his mind since she told him about the baby. After Sofia, he'd been afraid of strong passion, just as she had been afraid of depending on anyone after growing up the unwanted and illegitimate daughter of a famous actress.

Was she still afraid to depend on Salvatore?

Was that why she had reacted so strongly to her father's news and put the worst possible connotation on Salvatore's actions and motives? She had believed the worst of him because then he could not let her down as she had been let down so many times before.

She'd also been confusing unresolved emotional pain from her miscarriage with what she felt now.

So, she'd rejected him.

A rejection that had hurt.

If he didn't care about her, she could not hurt him. It followed, then, that he cared. Guilt thwarted would never have put that look on his face.

Giving up on getting any sleep with things unresolved between her and Salvatore, Elisa threw back the covers and climbed out of bed.

She went looking for Salvatore, but she didn't find him in their bedroom. So, she went downstairs. She tracked him down in the library. He was sprawled in a dark brown leather armchair, his shirt undone, his hand wrapped around an empty glass. He wasn't asleep though; his eyes were open and staring with bloodshot intensity at her.

"Salvatore?"

"What do you want, Elisa?" His perfect diction slurred the words together, so she could barely understand them.

So much for having a heart-to-heart talk. The man was drunk. Further evidence that she affected him deeply. He was way too strong and self-controlled to indulge in excess drinking on a whim.

"I want you to come to bed."

He blinked. "With you?"

"Yes."

He shook his head. "You do not want me in your bed."

"I changed my mind."

"You cannot. You hate me. You told me this." He sighed and looked at the empty glass in his hand as if trying to figure out how it had gotten there. "I must not forget."

"I don't hate you. I was angry, but I didn't mean it." She'd been unable to tell him she didn't want to marry him, but she'd certainly been capable of spouting enough hurtful words.

"You did not mean it." He set the glass on the table, but it caught the edge and fell to the floor.

Luckily, it did not break.

She ignored it because he was swaying to his feet and she wasn't sure he was not headed the same way as the glass.

To the floor.

He stopped in front of her and grasped her shoulders. She put her hands on his waist to steady him and then smiled at the thought of her puny strength holding up his massive body.

"You did not mean it," he repeated. He sounded as if he was having a hard time grasping the concept.

"Right. But I think we should talk about it in the morning."

"Why?"

"You're drunk."

His brow furrowed. "I do not drink excessively."

"Yes, I know, but this time you must have."

"You said you hated me." He said it much like a first-grader repeating his memory lesson and slightly bewildered by it.

"I didn't mean it," she repeated slowly, trying to get through the alcoholic stupor he appeared to be under, "and I want you to come to bed."

His bleary eyes brightened. "You will sleep in my bed."

"*Our* bed, and yes."

He let her lead him from the room, docile as a lamb. It almost scared her, this unknown Salvatore, but she liked it a little too. Usually he was so forceful, he would never let her undress him...at least not without doing some undressing of his own. This time he allowed her to pull his clothes off and press him toward the bathroom to brush his teeth before they went to bed.

Ten minutes later, she was wrapped snugly in his arms and he was snoring slightly. Salvatore never snored. It must be the alcohol. They would talk in the morning. She would make him tell her his real feelings once and for all.

Salvatore woke with little men in hobnailed boots dancing inside his head. His mouth tasted as if it were stuffed with wadded-up cotton and he needed to go to the bathroom.

That was his first sense of awareness.

His second told him that a small, warm and very naked body was curled into his and that body belonged to Elisa. Her hand was buried in the hair on his chest, pressed against his heart. One of her shapely legs was tucked between his own and her stomach pressed lightly against his morning erection.

It bobbed in awareness and he groaned.

She squirmed beside him.

He lifted his hand to his face, rubbing the rough stubble on his cheeks and wondering what this rapprochement meant.

How had she come to be in his bed? He remembered thinking briefly last night, during one burst of particularly drunken brainstorming, that he should go upstairs and carry her there. Had he done that?

Hazy memories of her undressing him did not fit with that scenario. Surely she would not have put him to bed if he had carried her into the room against her will. Then he remembered. She'd come to the library. They had talked. He couldn't remember the whole conversation, but certain things stood out.

He slid from the bed, careful not to wake her, the movement jarring his head. The tiny men in hobnailed boots each grew a second set of feet. He stifled another groan and headed to the *en suite*. He needed to shower, to shave, to drink some fluids and become at least semi-human before he could talk to Elisa and tell her what was in his heart.

She woke from a gentle brushing on the top curve of her breast. Her eyes fluttered open and she looked up. Salvatore sat beside her on the bed, freshly showered, looking much better than he had the night before. He'd donned a robe, but nothing else.

She looked down where the backs of his knuckles continued to brush back and forth against her soft flesh. The sheet was around her waist and her breasts were bare to his sight, a fact he had definitely noticed.

She reached for the sheet, feeling vulnerable all of a sudden.

He stayed her hand. "No, *amore*. You are so beautiful; it is a crime to cover such perfection."

The words were said so reverently that she could not take issue with them, but she curled her fingers around his wrist to stop the tantalizing movement of his hand. "We need to talk."

"*Sì.*" His dark brown gaze caught and held her own. "You said you do not hate me, is this the truth?"

"Yes."

"You were very angry last night. My thoughtlessness hurt you and for this I do not know how to make amends."

"You wanted to marry my sister."

"I did not."

He sounded so sure that she had to believe him.

"I don't understand."

"You scared me. The way I felt when I was around you scared me."

She shook her head back and forth on the pillow. "No. Nothing frightens you."

Not even gunmen. She would never forget how she had had to blackmail him into the vault.

"*Sì.* Scared. You evoked strong emotions I did not want."

"Because of Sofia."

"My first reaction to you eclipsed any feelings I ever had for her. You did not only threaten my self-control, you threatened my heart."

Her breath paused and then came out in a big whoosh. "That sounds as if you cared."

"I fell in love with you before you ever left Sicily, but I refused to admit it. Did not need to admit it. You allowed me to seduce you, gave me all of your spare time. I was happy."

"And then I told you I was pregnant."

"And I destroyed what we had because of fear, old wounds and a stupid misunderstanding."

"You kept trying to see me."

"I could not let you go. You are the other half of myself. Without you I am not half-alive, I am dead."

She shivered at the finality and sincerity of his words. He'd said he had fallen in love with her. "Do you still love me?"

"More than you can know, *amore*. More than I can ever say."

"But Annemarie…"

"Was a thought, an attempt at a smoke screen of my feelings."

"But I didn't know what you felt!"

"Not for you, for myself. I lied to myself and convinced myself what we had was merely physical, but I paid a price."

"The baby."

"And you. I lost my child and my woman in one fell swoop of my pride, in doing things in the wrong way."

She struggled into a sitting position, needing to touch him. He allowed her to put her arms around him, but he remained distant.

She kissed his hairy, muscular chest, reveling in

the scent of his skin and the warmth of it against her lips. "I care about you. I need you."

"How can you after all I have done?" His voice was hoarse with emotion. "Last night, you cried so much." The torment in his voice tore at her heart.

"Last night..." She paused, unsure how to go on. *"Sì?"*

"It was more than just what you thought about me last summer. It was as if a dam had burst and all the hurt I'd tried to ignore after losing the baby came out." She drew on the strength of having his warmth surrounding her and spoke a truth that had devastated her. "I didn't cry after the baby. There was no one to grieve with."

"I would have grieved with you."

Finally, she believed that was true and it healed wounds that had been gouged by his supposed indifference.

"I couldn't forgive you. Not then." She sighed, wishing he would put his arms around her, and nuzzled his chest some more. "And last night everything got all jumbled together."

His big body shuddered and then two strong arms locked around her in a hold that said he would never let her go. "I am glad you finally grieved, but I pray God you never know such pain again. It unmans me."

She shifted slightly and felt a growing hardness against her. "You don't feel unmanned."

"Do not tease. We have serious things to discuss."

"Like what?" she asked, all innocence.

He pulled back and glowered at her. "Like whether my love is returned, you little torment."

"I could never stop loving you, Salvatore."

"You tried."

"We had it all backwards."

"*Sì*, the honeymoon before the courtship."

She nodded.

"We have to fix this, to put it right."

She didn't know what he meant, but she soon learned. Salvatore spent the next week courting her in every way a man could court a woman. He escorted her to the auction, treating her like a date, leaving the security to his father, who had flown in to attend the sale of the crown jewels.

There were no problems and later she learned the men who had tried to rob Adamo Jewelers had not been fanatics at all. Just regular jewel thieves who'd had a tip-off on the early transport of the crown jewels. They had been caught in a net set by Salvatore's firm and were now facing long sentences in an Italian prison.

In the meantime, Salvatore brought her flowers, bought her beautiful jewelry, wrote her poetry that was terrible, but she would never tell him so, and refused to share their bed until after the wedding. She'd complained, saying he already considered her his wife, but he had remained firm.

She deserved a courtship and she would get it.

Their wedding was as big and loud as any Sicilian family could make it. It wasn't until they boarded his private jet to take off for their real honeymoon that they were alone.

She snuggled into his lap, her over-the-top, gorgeous wedding dress flowing around both of them. "You belong to me now."

"As you belong to me." And he meant it. The

acceptance she had craved her whole life, the legitimate place in the life of another, were hers with Salvatore. He adored her and wanted to be with her all the time. He needed her and had shown her in so many ways how real that need was, but nothing more so than the year he spent trying to get her back when she had walked away from the pain of her loss and left him behind.

"I love you." She kissed his throat right above the shirt points of his tux.

His arms tightened around her and his lips sought hers for a kiss that left her smiling and loopy with joy. "I love you, *amore,* always and forever. Never doubt it."

"How can I? I can feel it with every breath you take, every glance, every touch. Our love is like a living bond between us."

"*Sì.*" He pressed his hand over her womb. "Very alive."

EPILOGUE

A YEAR later Elisa led Salvatore across the threshold of a small cottage in the hills of Tuscany.

"So this is where you hid from me so well I could not find you."

She smiled and nodded. "Isn't it beautiful?"

It was a simple one-room abode with a bathroom, but the surrounding country was gorgeous.

"*Sì*, but not as beautiful as my two best girls." He looked down with adoration at the tiny baby in his arms. "She is so precious, *dolcezza*. Perfect."

"You're prejudiced."

His head came up and chocolate-dark eyes mocked her. "And you are not?"

She laughed rather than answer. He knew how besotted she was, with both her husband and her four-month-old baby daughter.

"So, who does this place belong to?"

"Me. Papa's mother gave it to me the year before she died. She said it was my place in this world, where I belonged without any stipulations or limitations."

He came to her then and put his arm around her, making a perfect circle of their small family. "Now I am that place for you, no?"

"Oh, yes. Now you are that place."

And would always be. Love had given her a place in his heart and his life that no one could ever take away.

She belonged.

REQUEST YOUR FREE BOOKS!

HARLEQUIN® *Presents*

2 FREE NOVELS PLUS 2 FREE GIFTS!

PASSION
GUARANTEED
SEDUCTION

HP06

HARLEQUIN *Presents*

GREEK TYCOONS

*They're the men who have
everything—except brides...*

Wealth, power, charm—what else could a
heart-stoppingly handsome tycoon need?

Now it's the turn of favorite Presents author

Trish Morey,

with her attention-grabbing romance

THE GREEK'S VIRGIN.

This tycoon has met his match, and he's decided
he has to have her...whatever it takes!

Buy this title in January!

**Look for more titles from this miniseries
coming in February & March!**

www.eHarlequin.com

HPGT0107